MONOLOGUE

Monologue

Hannes Bajohr

FROHMANN/OXOA

Monologue

I'm a 24-year-old straight male and I'm unattractive, and I'm pregnant, and I'm a big fat liar, so I'm at a loss, Dan, but I'm innocent, and I'm not sure how that works exactly, yet I'm effing scared, and I'm rare, I know, but I exist, yet I'm fine with this, because I'm an only child, male, born to a single mom, what's more, I'm a virgin at 30, which means that I'm a down-to-earth, normal fag like all the rest, on the other hand, I'm not, hence I'm a prime example, and I'm an adorable 270 pounds, so I'm going out of my mind, in addition to that, I'm a homo, hence I'm about to give up and become a nun or something, on the other hand, I'm a guy who does not find guys physically attractive, and I'm a feminine, submissive dyke, yet I'm a pretty hairy dude, so I'm not so sure, and I'm a little dominant, but nothing too out there, on the other hand, I'm a 22-year-old FTM, what's more, I'm a straight woman who hasn't had sex in five years, and I'm in a crisis, just as I'm an animal already—I'm a primate, like you, yet I'm actually kinda reluctant to say this out loud, because I'm serious, and I'm a 32 year-old Asian male living in Seattle, just as I'm also as horny as a 17-year-old, and I'm a vegetarian married to a meat eater, in a word, I'm a 28-year-old, professional, single woman, so I am an attractive college student, and I am a 20-year-old male who has a fetish that other people just don't understand, for I am an 18-year-old British queer girl who was recently involved with an older woman while visiting the United States, what's more, I'm not into it, though, and it's hurting our relationship, for I'm as GGG as girls get, but I'm one of those rare types who was sexually abused by an adult woman when I was a young girl, in addition to that, I'm constantly battling my weight, while he, through unswerving diligence (and good genes, I'm convinced), has a very cut bod, hence I'm submissive and prefer my partners to be

dominant, so I'm going to Barack Obama's
inauguration in Washington, D.C. on January
20, in a word, I'm a 21-year-old gay boy with a
kinky side that I keep pretty private, just as
I'm afraid I'll wind up with another Paul and
not a Peter, and I'm glad that my husband is
having great sex, but my health problems
leave me sexually unfulfilled, also I'm the het
white male engaged to Wedding Bell Blues,
although I'm not okay with that, in a word, I
am torn, because we both acknowledge that if
the situation were different, we would make
excellent life partners, and I'm GGG and
excited by trying out new-to-me stuff, and I'm
tired of all the perv, kink, bisexual dilemmas
in your column, so needless to say that I am
ashamed to be akin to you in any semblance,
and I am a 29-year-old straight male, and I am
a 23-year-old straight female, and I'm not
traumatized, just as I'm a 20-year-old woman
who in the past six months has been
masturbating frequently, sometimes three or
more times a day, but I am a female in a
relationship with a male, just as I'm often
cruised, and men have told me that I am
good-looking and have expressed interest in
me, so I'm happy, but I need help, also I'm not

only officially against sleeping with someone
under the age of consent, I'm really most
sincerely dead set against it, on the other
hand, I am a 47-year-old gay man who has a
desire to be humiliated and degraded—by a
straight guy, on top of that I'm 19, female, bi,
and have been with the same guy for a year,
for I'm an American man but I'm writing
from Canada, where my husband and I live,
and I am shocked that any newspaper would
publish your wicked commentary; you take 10
giant steps back for the whole of gay culture,
and I'm 25 now, also I'm sure your readers
would love to know the answers to all of these
questions, which means that I'm not worried
about health issues, as everything was safe,
also I'm a 23-year-old lesbian who's been in a
relationship with a bisexual woman, yet I am
also interested if she is fertile and wants to be
bred in front of hubby, and I'm a 25-year-old
woman who can only get off lying facedown
and rubbing my clit against a pillow, and I'm
old enough to remember when getting fucked
in the ass was considered a sex act, for I'm a
man who loves it when my girlfriend fucks me
with a strap-on, just as I am a heterosexual
male, but perennially single, and wanted to

help out other guys who have gotten bored
with Rosy Palm and her five sisters, and I'm
what was once quaintly called a woman of a
certain age who started reading your column
to broaden my horizons, and I am a 22-year-
old guy in Michigan, for I'm just not attracted
to my guy sexually, in a word, I'm a heavy
sleeper, so I guess I don't hear him pee into a
plastic liter bottle in the middle of the night,
yet I am really in love with her and could see
myself marrying her but I need to be assured
that I will get a blowjob at some point in my
life, hence I'm certainly more fond of him
than any other relationship I've been in, and
I'm a twentysomething freelancer, and I have a
barter relationship with a facility that lets me
work there for free, which means that I'm so
afraid I'm going to catch some kind of
infection from his tongue, so you can guess
that I'm fucking this random guy on the beach
when I look down to find that my dick is
covered with shit, also I'm a 45-year-old,
financially secure male with a BIG problem,
what's more, I'm a 26-year-old woman and a
devotee, which means that I am primarily
attracted to men with disabilities, just as I am
a 28-year-old straight woman who has been

dating a 24-year-old straight male for two
months, and I'm feeling like an emotionally
leotarded, sexually repressed teenager, on top
of that I'm bored, so I am a 22-year-old
female with a wonderful, caring, 21-year-old
boyfriend, and I'm still not happy with myself
naked—rapid weight loss due to health
problems does not a Britney body make, so
I'm gay, been gay for years now, and I want to
be with a man as a life partner, and I'm 21
years old and in a monogamous relationship,
but I am a 38-year-old married woman, so I'm
Being Selfish, yet I am a married white guy in
my 50s, which means that I'm going for
electrolysis now, and even though it's slower,
the results are 10 times better, which means
that I'm a 16-year-old male writing because of
an uncomfortable situation with my father,
and I'm trying to hold on to something
because this is just surreal, just as I'm actually
sitting on the beach as I write these words,
knocking back margaritas and watching my
boyfriend's tan lines come in, for I'm not just
interested in sex—I'd like to have a real
relationship, and I'm a top; she's a sub, and
I'm wondering whether you have any
thoughts on the male tendency when sharing

naughty photos to go straight for a close-up
shot of the penis, also I am a 21-year-old male
in a loving and committed relationship, hence
I'm a 37-year-old father, what's more, I'm
beginning to get a complex, in a word, I am
writing in response to your comments to
Chilled in Chicago, although I'm also
seriously missing the woman I thought would
be my wife, in addition to that, I'm a 29-year-
old single gay man with some major kinks:
I'm into bondage, diapers, and have a subby
fantasy life, on top of that I am a happily
married, also I'm a young heteroflexible guy
who has been a sugar baby for a handful of
wealthy older guys, hence I am fine with them
dating, but I have a few questions, yet I'm a
woman in my 20s, and I've been dating the
love of my life for two years now, but I am a
26-year-old straight girl and a virgin, although
I am sexually attracted to my English teacher
and I think she's attracted to me, on top of
that I'm a 29-year-old gay man, for I'm not
sure whether to be scared or amused, also I'm
a married male in my 40s who has recently
discovered the pleasure of drinking my wife's
pee, so I am a 23-year-old female, sexually
active for seven years, and I can't reach climax,

in a word, I'm disappointed, and I am a bi
man married to a straight woman for 10 years,
just as I am a 24-year-old female and my
husband is a 37-year-old male, so I'm a first-
year student at a university in Canada, on the
other hand, I am a gay male, so needless to
say that I'm a straight guy, a sophomore in
college, and I have a problem with girls, and
I'm pretty well-built, hence I am self-
conscious about my body and can only come
using a vibrator while looking at pictures of
women with nice boobs, also I'm not
embarrassed by it at all (I'm completely
uncloseted); I'd just rather talk about more
interesting things, but I'm a 28-year-old gay
man, hence I'm a 24-year-old woman who
just ended a five-year relationship, whereas I
am also a rape survivor, and I am a college-age
gay male, just as I'm at a loss for what to do,
but I'm hurt, also I'm a 25-year-old straight
male who's into big-dick porn, also I am 18
years old, so I am barely legal, and I'm not
talking about sadists who sexually torture
strangers, yet I'm a straight guy who has no
problems with the gay lifestyle, and I'm a
mostly closeted gay, having come out only to
some of my friends, but my best friend was

the first one I told, on top of that I'm hairy,
and I am a woman of muse, so I'm writing to
ask you to help me spread the word about an
issue close to my heart, which means that I
am an 18-year-old female college freshman, yet
I'm wondering if these feelings of annoyance
are normal in longer-term serious
relationships, on top of that I'm a good-
looking guy with a good job, so needless to say
that I'm a bi woman in my mid-20s in a great
monogamish relationship with my straight
boyfriend, and I am currently dating a guy
who is nice, funny, has a good dating résumé,
on the other hand, I am a 30-year-old woman,
so you can guess that I am a bi male in my
early 20s who until recently was in the closet,
on top of that I'm a hetero girl, and I'm going
to go out on a limb and declare my
homosexual union to be morally superior to a
lot of heterosexual marriages, and I'm going
nuts because I want it to be mutual and wild
like it was before, but I am a huge fan and
never thought that I would be writing you a
letter like this, and I'm a gay man in my 20s,
yet I'm studying the wonderful world of
engineering, although I am in a great
relationship with a very sexy and open-

minded woman, just as I'm not more attracted to overweight women than other women, but sometimes that type just does it for me, but I'm a 24-year-old straight guy, in a word, I am a 32-year-old heterosexual married man, on top of that I am sick over this situation, and I don't know what to do, just as I am hanging out at a friend's house and he is asleep, but I'm 20 now and dating a 41-year-old crossdresser, hence I am a straight 29-year-old guy and I've been into ball busting—having my balls kicked and stomped—since I was 14, on the other hand, I'm pretty sure that the solution is for me to jump my sexy boyfriend more often, and I am married for the second time, to a wonderful 42-year-old woman, which means that I'm sure you'll receive an avalanche of e-mail supporting ITMFA [Impeach the Motherfucker Already] lapel pins, T-shirts, and bumper stickers, yet I'm a woman in a relationship with an AMAZING guy for eight years, so you can guess that I am a 24-year-old woman who loves everything butt—except butthole, also I'm a 23-year-old straight male, on top of that I'm a guy in my late 30s and have been married for 12 mostly happy years, with three kids, which means that I'm worried that those interested in me would see me as a bottom, which simply isn't the case, so needless to say that I'm a pretty good-looking guy (former college athlete) and lately I've only been letting other good-looking guys suck me off, whereas I'm not sure if I can face my girlfriend of a year, which means that I'm a straight man with a bisexual wife, married a little over two years, whereas I'm not disgusted by pussy juice, I just want to keep things neat, in addition to that, I am a 27-year-old gay man, and that I'm grateful to my parents for handling these situations the way they did; I believe I'm a sexually well-adjusted adult as a result, and I'm bisexual, but not one of THOSE bisexuals, yet I'm gay and so is my insanely attractive boyfriend, whereas I'm a 20-year-old female girl, and I am sure you will get a lot of mail on this one, on the other hand, I am gay and I have a brother who's gay, although I'm not running this contest to get laid, but I'm a straight 18-year-old girl, and I have been dating my boyfriend for eight months, and I'm certainly no role model, but am I crazy to feel guilt for not being openly poly, also I am a 27-year-old female, and I think I have a sexual dysfunction, so I'm a straight 22-year-old male, just as I'm not, but I am interested in expanding my limits by dressing up and serving a gay couple as their sissymaid, on the other hand, I am a 25-year-old lesbian, so needless to say that I'm writing about the Choicer Challenge you've issued to all the bigots out there who say that being gay is a choice, on top of that I'm a 28-year-old woman, and I am a straight man, and I'm a 26-year-old lesbian 18 months out of an eight-year relationship, and I am Asian, you see, yet although I think I'm pretty stable and have a decent body, Gay.com has been a very bad experience for me, on top of that I'm afraid this person will out me and I will be harassed at best and fired at worst, although I'm not into the dicks per se, Dan, but I'm a college grad who's having a tough time meeting girls, and I am a 21-year-old girl who is very much in love with a 24-year-old boy, hence I'm a 32-year-old bi gal into both sub and dom roles with men, also I'm a 22-year-old straight male, and I am a young, straight male—but I have this obsession with male-on-male dino-dragon porn, so I'm happy, but I have a kink and I'm wondering how I could safely explore it, on top of that I am still willing to do everything with my partner and make sure she is satisfied, so needless to say that I'm confused, because I'm a male college student who's working to become a teacher, whereas I'm a man who just got out of a two-year relationship with a great girl, in addition to that, I'm madly in love with my girlfriend, whereas I'm a gay guy who has had a crush on a straight construction worker who has been working across the street from where I work for a year now, yet I am a 26-year-old female, and I'm 22, gay, male, and have been out for six months, and I'm going NUTS, Dan, all alone, masturbating to half-assed medical fetish websites, in addition to that, I am not invited because he doesn't like me and I don't like him, and I am a straight male 22-year-old who has always had an interest in a girl's bare feet, on top of that I am a 19-year-old gay man in a relationship with a handsome, nice guy, whereas I'm not asexual, on the other hand, I'm going to stuff it down the memory hole and pretend it didn't happen, what's more, I am dating a man who is kind, considerate, and mature, and sexy to boot, but I'm attractive, fit, over average height for a man, and passable—although I am quite slim and look like I'm about 17, and I am a homosexual because I touch myself, which means that I am also afraid he will not be able to handle the reality of the humiliation, whereas I'm a 20-year-old female college student, and I have a boring history of serial monogamy, whereas I'm a twentysomething married trans guy in an openish marriage, hence I'm very fond of Michael Bailey, on the other hand, I am a 29-year-old single straight man, yet I'm lucky he's still hard when I get out of the bathroom, on the other hand, I'm a nerdy guy, definitely not muscular or athletic, so needless to say that I am only 20 years old and I want to live my life and not be tied down all the time with some controlling guy, hence I am looking for hetero femme dom porn videos aimed at women, what's more, I am a 24-year-old Gay male, for I'm not a lesbian, but it had always been a fantasy of mine to be dominated by a woman, tied up, and, you know, other stuff, what's more, I'm a 26-year-old woman who lives with two other women around the same age, and I'm still sweating it out here, six days before the election, incapable of thinking of

anything else, literally sick with worry, also I
am in my mid-30s, my brother and his
girlfriend are in their early 40s, also I'm a
27-year-old man with cerebral palsy, and a
longtime reader, who is hoping you can help
me, on the other hand, I'm a 37-year-old
straight male and I've never had a girlfriend,
yet I'm talking about first-time encounters
here; obviously as a relationship develops,
partners can talk more openly about these
matters, just as I am 20 years old and have no
intention of running for public office, so if
there is any time to do something like being in
porn it is now, on top of that I'm a porn-
positive woman in my 30s, and I'm writing to
you to settle a dispute between my husband
and me, what's more, I'm a straight guy, and I
have had gay friends try the same shit on me,
and it always gives me the creeps and ruins
the friendship, hence I'm gay and my
boyfriend and I have known him since college,
but I'm only 20, and I am really in love with
this boy, so obviously I am hurt and confused
by this, what's more, I am a hetero female, but
one of my biggest fantasies is for a guy to
dress up in women's underwear, so needless to
say that I'm an 18-year-old male, and I am

certain I will end up getting busted (at least my parents were honest about fucking other people), and I'm a gay college student who's into bondage and kink, for I am an 18-year-old straight guy, on top of that I am a 28-year-old, post-op transsexual woman, also I'm a 50-year-old gay guy and I've always found anal to be painful, on the other hand, I am not looking to cheat on anyone, yet I am a bit older and have always been interested in queer culture and history, also I'm an 18-year-old male who is weird in the way of a bit of crossdressing and pegging, for I'm a straight, 22-year-old female, which means that I'm comfortable with my sexuality, and I'm a straight girl who hates all the slang terms for vagina, in addition to that, I'm straight and I'm pretty close to doing that, what's more, I'm on a kick-ass coed Ultimate Frisbee team, but I am a 15-year-old male with a question—what is proper etiquette regarding pubic hairs, also I'm really guilt-tripping myself about it, for I'm 28 years old and live in the Midwest, in a word, I am a 27-year-old black woman, whereas I am open to the possibility of a three-way, for I'm a happy fiftysomething straight female sub in a D/s relationship, so

you can guess that I'm afraid my current
friends will find out that I'm a virgin and be
outraged that I've been lying to them, hence
I'm afraid this loser is going to destroy all
that, for I'm convinced I never really learned
how to flirt, yet I am a 22-year-old straight
female, but I also sleep with women, on the
other hand, I am a 31-year-old gay man in a
new relationship, in addition to that, I am in a
heterosexual relationship, whereas I'm sure
I've met gay men, but how do you approach
such a subject, in addition to that, I'm a guy
who can't orgasm during oral sex, in a word, I
am a straight man, married with kids,
although I'm 24 years old and still a virgin,
also I'm a very normal person, so you can
guess that I am not sure how often people
together this long have sex, but for us it is
about once every three or four weeks, what's
more, I am a 23-year-old woman without
medical insurance who relies on Planned
Parenthood, so I am a 21-year-old bisexual
female, also I'm a 29-year-old gay guy who's
not sure where to find what I'm looking for, in
addition to that, I'm ready, although I am
jealous of gay culture on this score, but
bellyaching serves no purpose, and I'm sure

you're aware that Ashton Kutcher has a new show on MTV called Punk'd in which celebrities are subjected to pranks, although I'm not saying you shouldn't do this, and I'm confused, also I am a single, thirtysomething female who has been having a long-term affair with a married man, on the other hand, I'm 32 year-old gay man into medical restraints and sneakers, and I'm curious why I relate more easily to my straight friends and am increasingly uncomfortable with my gay friends, also I'm a hipster girl and stroking the silky texture of a nice stretched-out set of earlobes gets me insanely wet, so you can guess that I'm not stupid (I'm a physician), but I can't figure this one out, in a word, I'm not exactly bursting with confidence myself, either, but I tried my best to be a loving and supportive boyfriend, for I'm a newly lactating woman who would like to recoup some of the many expenses associated with having a child, so I am most likely very naive, but one company's (Natural Measures) website looks quite professional, and I'm a slut, too, and I am certain of my sexual orientation: I did quite a bit of experimenting with beautiful women, but they did nothing for me, and I'm

a 28-year-old woman, on the other hand, I am
honest, hard working, attractive, and fun to be
with, just as I'm wondering if there are places
that sell human breast milk to fetishists (I'm
sure they're out there), in addition to that, I'm
a straight 18-year-old female, a senior in high
school, and I'm still a virgin, for I am one of
those straight girls who like to make out with
other girls when I am drunk, yet I'm a
45-year-old black gay man and I hope not to
come off preachy: Please don't imitate thugs,
and I'm genuinely impressed by their website,
which means that I'm driven, I'm smart, I'm
going to India as a volunteer this summer, and
I'm handsome, just as I'm his grad student
and I'm gay, whereas I am a heterosexual
woman, in a word, I am a 40-ish married
straight woman living in New York, so I'm
well aware of how sexual kids can be, hence
I'm a married woman in my 40s who has
lately admitted that I hate being penetrated
by a dick, for I am thinking about becoming a
professional escort (transvestite), also I'm
tired of my baby girl; I want my husband
back, so needless to say that I'm a firm
believer in truthful, open communication, but
not in this area, in a word, I'm doing all I can

to keep his nuts drained—basically, I'm doing
for him what your right hand does for you, on
the other hand, I'm a straight woman who
loves my boyfriend, but sex isn't a priority for
me, although I'm disfigured, not stupid, and
I'm sick of CIAW types insisting with one
breath that sex and sexual exclusivity are
hugely important, on the other hand, I am a
bisexual woman in a nonmonogamous
marriage with a lesbian, so needless to say
that I'm a 27-year-old gay man in a three-year
relationship, whereas I'm only mildly
experienced (I've had just one boyfriend), and
I'd like to think I'm a nice guy, which means
that I'm a 23-year-old female in a
monogamish relationship—thank you for
that word, but I'm a sexually adventurous guy
for I had an uncomfortable reaction to your
advice for TRADE, the guy who wants to be a
hustler for day, on the other hand, I'm a loud
fucker, just like the partner of the woman
who wrote in recently, so I'm totally into him,
and it's amazing, in addition to that, I am also
wary of folks who call themselves devotees,
for I'm a 40-year-old white male who has
been with over 100 women, and I'm writing to
you on behalf of all the gals out there with

sensitive tits, in addition to that, I am a
33-year-old married male who has a WAM—
wet and messy—fetish, so needless to say that
I'm a breeder boy still happily in love with my
breeder chick after 10 years of marriage, and
I'm going to cut straight to the chase: I am a
good-looking 20-year-old with a boyfriend I
love dearly, and I am a 26-year-old gay man
living in Boston, also I'm a 24-year-old
straight, married female, whereas I am not
turned on by men at all, but I do enjoy the
enthusiastic BJs when combined with straight
porn, also I am too ashamed to ask a single
soul in the world these questions, but I'm a
strait actor and I have more strait actor
friends than gay actor friends, and I am all for
that in theory, but I have a hard time
emotionally, so you can guess that I'm gonna
be a writer, a good one, also I am healthy, and
I'm fairly certain that no other friends of his
know about his dressing up, with the
exception of old girlfriends/lovers, and I'm
gay but I'm just a normal guy, so I'm a
24-year-old male who has been out for 11
years, for I'm 21, he's 42, a big, hairy daddy
type, in addition to that, I am very insecure,
and I am a 43-year-old mother of three,

married for almost 20 years, but I'm a 21-year-
old heterosexual male, which means that I'm
19 and closeted, in a word, I'm a straight
woman who has been married for 10 years,
and I'm a wannabe sex columnist, so I'm a
married 28-year-old male, and I'm so
confused, because I don't know what to do,
and I'm a 22-year-old male from Canada and
in a long-term relationship, on the other
hand, I'm worried it might already be out
there that I'm gay, and I am convinced there
are thousands of men out there as deluded as
that guy, so needless to say that I'm her only
friend and she doesn't have anyone to tell
things to, whereas I'm a guy in my early 20s,
nearing my fourth anniversary dating a girl
my age, just as I'm into fetish SM, so I'm open
to the possibility of a threesome, but my
boyfriend isn't, which means that I'm a
student at UW Madison and I have a serius
[sic] problem, and I'm not a cheater, but I'm
in my mid-40s, and I'm surprised she
remembers to breathe in her sleep, on top of
that I'm not an instigator, although I have
tried a few times and have been rejected, so
I'm hoping you can give me some advice,
what's more, I am otherwise good-looking

and in shape—but what does that matter, on top of that I am torn, and I'm in my 30s, male, married, and bisexual, so you can guess that I am now in a great one, but I have a hard time believing/trusting that nothing bad will happen, which means that I'm a high-school girl with big problems, and I'm now a professor in my mid-30s at a small liberal arts college, and guess what, so I'm also not a NO, on top of that I am a 20-year-old gay male living in Philadelphia, in addition to that, I am hardly attracted to him, physically or emotionally, and I have no desire to reciprocate, hence I am furious that this woman would have me remove my oldest, closest, most important friend from my wedding party, because I'm a happily married woman, so I'm considering asking my sister to out me to my mom so that maybe she'll be done screaming and yelling by the time she arrives, and I am a 27-year-old straight male, and I'm all for getting a second opinion, which means that I am white and my fantasies involve my future wife having sex with well-endowed black men, and I'm a 16-year-old bisexual guy, in addition to that, I am a straight male, and I'm pretty sure I'd be less likely to come between the Bush girls, Jenna and Barbara, although I am used to cunts and like the ins and outs of them, the taste, the smell, and everything that comes with them, so I'm head over heels for this girl, and I don't want to come between her and her best friend, because I'm a lousy gift-giver but a decent mate, what's more, I'm not very experienced, although I'm extremely kinky and he's not, and we have some difficulties meeting each other's needs, in a word, I'm a 28-year-old guy who was broken up with via text by a girl I had been dating for two months, and I'm a SWM, 28, somewhat smart, and an accomplished jailhouse lawyer, on the other hand, I'm in great shape, my amazing ass gets hit on all the time, because I'm open-minded, also I'm a 27-year-old gay man, so needless to say that I am uncircumcised, and the opening at the end of my foreskin is not large enough for the head of my penis to pass through, in addition to that, I'm a 30-year-old straight guy 18 months into a relationship with a 30-year-old bi woman, and I am a Pennsylvania voter and I, too, am appalled at what Senator Rick Santorum represents in the U.S, in addition to that, I'm sure you've

addressed this qualm many times: I'm
wondering if it's bad that I use porn to
masturbate, for I am not looking to turn her
into an anal fanatic or a sloppy blowjob
queen, but rather for her to put aside her
preconceived notions and give some things a
try by embracing them fully, so needless to say
that I'm a single, 22-year-old, adorable lesbian
living in Chicago, although I am married and
my husband cannot function sexually
anymore, but I do love him and we have been
married for more than 25 years, so needless to
say that I'm attracted to D, he is sweet, hot,
and funny, but he's obviously gay, and I'm
frustrated because I know it's not his fault,
but I sometimes feel that he isn't putting in
enough effort to try to bottom for me, and I'm
going to do this: That's not in question, also I
am just an adult having sexy fun with other
consenting adults, but I am obsessed with my
girlfriend sitting on my face, so I can eat her
out while my nose penetrates her, so needless
to say that I'm 22 years old and gay; my
roommate is 28 years old and straight, and I
am not questioning my sexuality, I'm not bi, I
have zero desire to date women, just as I'm
sure there are more people than just me who

need to talk about this, but I'm almost 10 years older than you and I'm still battling my inner/giddy 13-year-old, in addition to that, I am a 27-year-old hetero female, whereas I'm a 200 percent straight guy, married with children, and I'm a college student with a crush on a TA (Teaching Assistant), because I am a 22-year-old female, and I am an 18-year-old straight male, and I'm not afraid of exploring caves or rappelling off cliffs, but I'm a total wimp when it comes to interacting with a potential mate, so I am gay, 22 years old, and have only been sexually active for about two years, and I am a pediatric nurse, so he brought his concerns to me, but the questions are totally outside my area of expertise, whereas I'm also single, in a word, I am way too critical, and he has erectile dysfunction, aka issues getting and staying hard, on the other hand, I'm well aware that there is a large range of dick sizes for men, but I'm only about two inches when erect, and I'm having a hard time concentrating on the sex-advice thing at the moment because the MOTHERFUCKING election is six days away, and I'm so crazed with lust that I'm having a hard time thinking straight, because

I am a 43-year-old female who's in a six-month relationship with a 26-year-old male, but I'm afraid that if I tell him how much I like it, he'll think I'm freaky, but I'm also afraid of not getting the spankings I crave, what's more, I am a high-functioning regular heroin user (not quite an addict), and I feel constantly compelled to hide my drug use, and I am extremely frustrated, although I'm a 31-year-old man and my girlfriend is 28, in addition to that, I'm 6′3 and she's a foot shorter, whereas I'm in a monogamous heterosexual relationship, on the other hand, I'm a 47-year-old man and my wife is 49, so needless to say that I'm a pretty quiet Midwestern woman currently wracked by a guilty Catholic conscience, also I'm in my mid-40s, straight, never married, and I'm stuck in a mentally and sometimes physically abusive relationship with a total cunt, because I'm a gay man who never experimented with girls when I was younger, which means that I'm a big fan, on the other hand, I'm a straight married guy and I don't like porn, so I am a woman in a relationship with a woman, which means that I'm not too bad off down there, but I want more, and I'm a straight 32-year-old woman who has been in a monogamous relationship with a guy for two years, in a word, I'm 25, I'm virgin, and I find it quite difficult to relate with girls, on the other hand, I'm a 24-year-old gay male in a three-year relationship with a man I love, and I am black, and if she were using the word nigger, I would call her on it and raise issue with our HR department, and I'm comfortable with that aspect of myself, but other people don't need to know, and I am starting to wonder if this is too good to be true, and I'm writing about the premature ejaculation guy in last week's column who wanted tricks for guys who are uncut and too sensitive, although I am a 26-year-old female who likes anal sex, because I'm about to move in with my boyfriend of four years, so you can guess that I'm a 30-year-old bi girl and have been with my girlfriend for nearly 10 years, also I'm familiar enough with your writing to know that you're not a huge devotee of the bear scene, but I'm a girl from Austria currently seeing a guy who likes to tie me up and gag me, so I'm interested in trying e-stim but I'm wary, whereas I'm trying to be GGG, but now it feels like every fuck needs to be a rape

scene, complete with choking, and I'm a
21-year-old female college student going to
school on the East Coast, although I am a
relatively experienced woman and I have
never encountered anything like this — he is
ALWAYS hard, yet I'm not, but I am not
ashamed of being HIV-positive, just as I'm an
18-year-old guy with an awesome kinky
girlfriend, which means that I'm a 23-year-old
gay male, but I am married to a man who is
into BDSM, so I'm waiting for the right person,
and it just hasn't happened yet, also I am
worried that my boyfriend will lose interest
when I quit smoking, and I'm so desperate
that I'm almost willing to pay for it, so
needless to say that I am to the point where I
feel like I am going to start cheating on him
and I don't want to do that, in a word, I'm
unemployed in Oregon and trying to come up
with simple ways to make rent, which means
that I'm being nice this week and, shit, man,
your father just died, because I'm a straight
guy who recently got out of a long-term
relationship, and I'm just afraid, so I'm a
22-year-old gay man, so needless to say that I
am happily married to a great woman, in
addition to that, I'm a straight guy in my early

30s with an amazing girlfriend of two years, just as I'm still horrified, so I am not asking the same of her: She does not have to sleep with other people to keep me in her life, also I'm a 19-year-old FTM who identifies as queer, but I am seriously disgusted because he puts the condiments back into the refrigerator when he's finished, and I'm a gay man in my late 20s who has been trying to deal with an attraction to young boys since I hit puberty, in a word, I'm not lonely in the sense of not having friends or family, because I have a lot of both, but I'm kind of freaked out by how not freaked out I am, and I am now suspended from my employment and may be dismissed, and I'm a young lesbian, although I am at risk for kidney failure, nerve damage, amputations, heart disease, stroke, and blindness—all at 25, so I am seeking your personal expertise, and I'm also queer, just as I'm afraid to tell her, on top of that I'm wondering because each time I hear about Rick Warren, I can't get past the name of his church, also I'm a 20-year-old female college student living with my 23-year-old boyfriend, and I am stuck, which means that I am a 21-year-old male with a wonderful girlfriend,

although I'm also a young husband who's gone
a few years past your recommended date for
laying down his kink cards, yet I'm not crazy,
and I am so embarrassed and insecure about
my hairiness that I'm afraid to undress in
front of a man, but I'm a 19-year-old
heterosexual female, because I'm a 26-year-old
guy in a polyamorous relationship, yet I am
the father of a recently out 18-year-old gay
boy, just as I am living with a man whom I
deeply love, and I'm a 23-year-old bi dude
seeing a guy who is intelligent and attractive,
just as I'm a lesbian, and my girlfriend is
bisexual and wants to have a three-way with a
man, so needless to say that I'm 20, gay, and I
just moved to the big city, on the other hand, I
am a male in an eight-year het relationship,
and I'm concerned that he's degrading me,
hence I'm especially interested in knowing
how many of us are muff divers, also I'm
wondering how best to address this, in a
word, I am a 35-year-old man who loves to
have sex with big women, but I am a 29-year-
old lesbian, so I'm worried because she is in
love with me, but I am not in love with her,
what's more, I am a queer lady in my 20s, and
I'm not surprised you didn't get complaints

from straight men about your comment that
all straight men want to fuck other women,
for I'm sure they do, because I'm a gay college
student, and I really like the guy I'm seeing,
also I am not sure how I feel about her getting
fucked by someone else, even if she's fucking
me at the same time, although I'm aware of
my own fetishes and kinks, and I'm confident
sharing them, on top of that I'm wondering
how safe this might be, yet I'm 21, male, in
good shape, and have been jerking off with a
death grip since I was 10, and I'm genderqueer
and do not look like a girl, so I am also
growing increasingly frustrated, on top of that
I'm straight so I don't know too much about
meeting gay guys in particular, and I'm an
early-40s gal living in the Midwest, just as I
am a full-time student and I need his help,
although I am a bi woman happily married to
a straight man, and we both participate in hot
sexy times with other women during
threesomes, but I'm really nervous about
having sex, becuase I am a 30-year-old
woman, although I'm a lesbian, and I am in
love, he gives a great blowjob, and I'll stay
with him no matter what, although I am a
bisexual female in a polyamorous relationship

with a bisexual male, and I'm sorry if my
English is wrong, but I'm a 31-year-old
woman, and my boyfriend and I are starting
to experiment with pegging, so needless to say
that I'm surprised at you, Dan, and I am
actually repulsed by my body, also I'm a
straight guy with conventional tastes in
women, so I'm getting bored and worried, and
I'm pretty uncomfortable topping my
boyfriend—he's always been the top, and I'm
nervous about doing it wrong, because I'm a
Canadian 25-year-old gay man in a four-year
relationship with a 22-year-old, so I am
ashamed of my father for doing it and I'm
even more ashamed of myself for not
preventing it, so needless to say that I'm
punting this one to you: What constitutes
virginity, for I'm a 31-year-old lesbian, and I'm
considering spying on her with a hidden
surveillance cam, on the other hand, I'm sure
I'm not alone in this sentiment, and I'm a
longtime reader who thought I'd never have a
reason to write since I'm universally known as
the good girl, yet I am a 23-year-old female
whose boyfriend has a piss fetish, so you can
guess that I'm a mid-40s gay man in a LTR
with a man I love very much, for I am in love

but miserable, yet I'm a 28-year-old woman in a relationship for 3.5 years with a wonderful man, also 28, and I'm very happy we are getting married, on the other hand, I'm a 41-year-old, very attractive, happily married woman, and I'm sure you've got a fair share of mail to go through, so I'll make this as quick as I can, but I'm a hetero guy in my late 20s, and I'm having a private lunch with my coworker soon, yet I'm a straight guy, and my first girl was very experienced—she was proud to say she'd been with at least 30 guys before me, which means that I'm good-looking, outdoorsy, adventurous, and free-spirited, and I'm sure you've answered a question like this before or have refused to answer on principle, but..., in a word, I'm not sure if he ever knew my last name, on the other hand, I'm NOT looking for softcore bondage pictures of men, or any other gay porn, also I am a straight 21-year-old female and have been with my boyfriend on and off for two years, and I'm a 20-year-old female virgin, which means that I'm a 35-year-old GGG married male with a 33-year-old not-so-GGG wife, in a word, I'm a straight white boy of 25 who is very excited about Obama's

victory and the landslide in Congress, so you
can guess that I am more sexually fulfilled
than I have been in a decade, on top of that
I'm dominant; she's submissive, and I'm an
under-30, good-looking, boy-next-door type
who is into fisting guys, yet I'm sort of
sensitive, in a word, I'm not naive, and I don't
expect my boyfriend not to look at porn, but I
am so angry, I can't imagine staying, although
I am a het husband, and I am a straight and,
dare I say it, vanilla woman who met a
straight man who somewhat reminds me of
Clark Kent, whereas I'm not bi, and I'm 22
years old and I am NOT ashamed of who I am,
for I am a closet crossdresser, but I'm also
GGG: I satisfy her fantasies too, and I'm just
wondering what lies in store for me and
whether there's any hope, so I'm gay and
single, said Bryn, and I've gone out on a few
dates with people I met at work, for I am a
straight 26-year-old male with a sexy,
adventurous girlfriend, and I'm thin and
traditionally good-looking, and I'm all for
seizing ecstasy in the present while exorcising
the horrors of your past, hence I am going to
get it as soon as possible so I can better
understand myself, yet I'm a 23-year-old gay

male who's been following the Rick Santorum
scandal, and I'm a 22-year-old woman with a
21-year-old boyfriend of 11 months, so I'm still
unable to admit my sexuality to my friends,
teammates, classmates, and hallmates, and I'm
a 27-year-old straight guy, what's more, I'm a
17-year-old girl and, in most aspects, I'm
confident with myself, my identity, and my
body, so needless to say that I'm not ugly, but
I'm in therapy and on medication, and even
still it's really difficult for me to wrap my head
around sex with new people, just as I'm a
32-year-old female, for I'm just saying, know
thyself a tad better, on top of that I'm not
asking him to let me fuck him or become his
lover; I just want to suck his dick occasionally,
because I'm 21 and I've always had trouble
coming during sex, no matter the position,
size of the guy, etc., what's more, I'm a woman
whose super-hetero boyfriend is quite shy
and needs to build trust before he can open
up to someone, although I'm a cute, mostly
straight, twentysomething, single, and (safely)
sexually active woman, what's more, I can't
believe this is why I'm finally writing you, and
I'm happy in my relationship, I have no plans
to leave, but I don't want to be married, for

I'm sure your readers would appreciate some
knowledgeable and well-reasoned advice on
the issue of bestiality, whereas I'm not ready,
which means that I'm one of your female
friends who's strayed from the path of True
Lesbianism, and I am now willing to give 110
percent to fix it, but I'm scared to talk to a
counselor about this because I don't want to
freak my parents out, because I'm in my 40s
and straight, and for most of my adult life, I
have suffered from complete sexual
dysfunction with partners, although I am
attracted to ladies with attractive lady feet,
and I am very interested in trying anal sex and
I have a willing partner, but I am 27, and I am
embarrassed, on the other hand, I'm also a
sadist, so I'm sure a few wet-suit fetishists
were at Folsom this year, along with guys in
gas masks and people in rubberized shorts,
yet I am a 29-year-old male with a fetish for
snapping pictures of women's legs and feet in
nylons, for I'm married to one and I'm madly
in love with her, what's more, I'm currently in
a relationship with a guy, and I am NOT
submissive in the relationship; we're very
much equals, in addition to that, I'm sure it's
her; I recognize a birthmark, and the position

she's in is one of her favorites, although I am a
20-year-old female college student who is still
living at home, but I'm convinced there are a
lot of older women out there who prefer
younger men, because I'm a 33-year-old
straight woman, married for 10-plus years to
an awesome guy, in a word, I am so
uncomfortable with this idea, so I am a
25-year-old lesbian, on the other hand, I am a
straight male, married to a woman for 25
years, yet I'm taking great pleasure in
exploring you sexually, and you look great in
that saddle, hence I am not bored sexually or
mentally, so I am extremely happy except for
one thing: I am a virgin, and I plan on
remaining one until the wedding night, and I
am a 22-year-old bisexual male who goes to a
small, prestigious liberal-arts college in the
Midwest, yet I am a very single, 41-year-old,
African American butch lesbian who does not
smoke cigarettes, drink alcohol, nor use drugs,
although I am a mostly straight, 22-year-old
woman, what's more, I'm an actor in New
York City, so I'm a 27-year-old man in a two-
year relationship with a 26-year-old woman,
yet I'm married and a mother and he's my
husband's friend, and I am familiar with his

work, in addition to that, I'm 18 years old, dating a 24-year-old, and I have a proposal, because I'm a straight woman in a monogamous, long-distance relationship with a straight man, which means that I'm hoping that she will experiment with being a lesbian and realize that she wants me back, because I'm a GGG woman and I'm fat, which means that I am a 23-year-old straight male, and I'm a cad for writing this, of course, yet I am way more attracted to girls than guys, but I can't shake these thoughts, so you can guess I'm a 26-year-old straight guy, just as I'm deeply confused about this, for I am a 28-year-old straight girl two years into my first marriage, which means that I'm a 29-year-old hetero male considering breaking up with my sweet GGG girlfriend of five years, because I am a 22-year-old woman, generally happy, but I have a problem with cheating, although I'm writing not for advice, but to open up a discussion, on top of that I'm writing for confirmation that this community exists, and I am wondering if by denying this kink I am being unfair or, worse yet, leaving him feeling unsatisfied in the way my ex made me feel, although I am a 26-year-old gay man who is obsessed with feces, and I am concerned not only that we are waking up my neighbors, but that we may find ourselves on the receiving end of a noise complaint, on the other hand, I'm sorry this happened to her, also I'm a straight guy in my late 20s, yet I'm a lesbian in a committed relationship, but looking for a bit of specific action, and I am concerned that he is unable to get off or feel a great amount of pleasure for the lack of friction, just as I am asking you, I suppose, for some advice, whereas I'm a 30-year-old straight woman, and I've been with my male partner for four years, but I'm a straight male in my early 30s, so it was about time, although I'm a 24-year-old straight female in a relationship, and I'm a 40-year-old gay man who has his life fairly together (career, home, etc.), but I'm trying not to wind up on the streets of L.A., because I'm not physically accustomed to getting off with anything but my hand, so I'm sure you're no stranger to hate mail, being an openly gay sex-advice columnist, but I hope you get fan mail too, because I'm gay, although I am a 21-year-old straight male, on top of that I'm good for about 15 minutes, because the pressure my wife puts on my nutsack gets to

be too much, so needless to say that I'm also
completely turned on by it, because I'm a
19-year-old bisexual female, and my current
girlfriend and I have been together about
three months, and I'm miserable, and I'm a
19-year-old bisexual male, so I'm a gay boy
who's always been versatile, on top and on the
bottom, switching things up, and I'm writing
because I need to ask someone what to think
right now, although I am a 25-year-old gay
man, yet I am a straight 24-year-old female
who has known my fiancé since freshman year
of college, in a word, I am desperately in need
of your help, but I'm sorry for snooping, also
I'm a 26-year-old heterosexual male in a
relationship with a 25-year-old female, and I
just got a blowjob from (and gave a half-assed
one to) a transsexual male-to-female
prostitute, and I'm having some doubts about
his honesty, although I'm a forgiving mom,
but it sounds like he's being a doormat, on the
other hand, I'm a 24-year-old guy, but I am
torn about what I should do, also I'm not
sexually experienced, but I am totally in love
with my new man and I want to drive him
wild with desire, which means that I'm a
31-year-old genderqueer in Brooklyn with a

large family on Long Island, whereas I am a 16-year-old female, and I'm 23 years old, single, and have no control over my penis (which is easily noticed when erect), and I'm a submissive gay man, whereas I'm a man who recently started seeing a wonderful woman, also I'm not even gonna look at porn, because the production of it involves child exploitation, on top of that I'm wondering if you know of any procedures, perhaps surgical, that would allow for the lengthening of the tongue, because I'm a single male in my mid-30s who over the years developed an incapacitating fetish, whereas I am a kinky, youthful 72-year-old guy, and I am a 24-year-old male, and I am perfectly happy being a male, on top of that I'm a 23-year-old bi woman, but I am a straight 25-year-old woman, although I've been dating my boyfriend for four years, yet I'm scared to because I'm scared he will be disappointed, whereas I am a 30-year-old cross-dresser who enjoys the occasional fantasy role-reversal in bed, so I'm a 23-year-young woman, and I've been with my boyfriend for more than five years, but I am not attracted to my cat, on the other hand, I am a 24-year-old straight girl,

which means that I'm not going to dun him
for child support, but I'd let him be as
involved as he wants to be—pictures, visits,
moving in together, so you can guess that I am
a 35-year-old partnered gay man, and I'm all
for gay marriage and adoption and all that
stuff, but I am completely traumatized by this
entire situation, and I nevertheless want to be
completely dominated by a woman, which
means that I am a 22-year-old bisexual female,
and I have a boyfriend who I love, in a word,
I'm sure many of those girls are more
attractive than me, and I am totally self-
reliant, but I'm GGG, so I mulled it over and
decided that I am not comfortable with that,
on the other hand, I'm a 25-year-old male, and
I am NOT going to cheat on my boyfriend, but
I don't know what to do, which means that
I'm pretty sure I had no sexuality at all before
my mid-to-late teens, and I'm satisfied that
Aldridge was alone, although I'm not sure if I
should approach him about this or not, and
I'm a fairly balanced guy, but I still feel the
urge to get out and be with other guys I find
more attractive, what's more, I'm glad you
finally explained the Hey, Faggot greeting, so
you can guess that I'm in my mid-20s and

recently started sleeping with a coworker who
is in his late 40s, hence I am jealous of the
way he treats and talks to his dog, but I'm
inclined to believe him, because it took him
quite a while to get to the point of just being
willing to strap me to the bed and jerk me, yet
I'm a female in my early 20s and have been
seeing a really great guy for a few months, on
top of that I am also hot, vain, in shape, and
kinky as all hell, and I'm 33 and for many
years I've felt a strong attraction to my
mother, and for that reason have never dated,
hence I'm a 25-year-old straight male with a
wonderful girlfriend, in a word, I am
attractive, confident, and I've been told I'm
the fantasy girl of every lover's dreams more
than once, and I'm a producer with a
Chicago-based production company started
by a handful of former Oprah show
producers, so you can guess that I am flirted
with frequently in my daily life, and I find
myself increasingly desperate for even a small
taste of sexual intimacy, but I am a 22-year-
old woman who got drunk with some friends
and downloaded some sick porn, and I'm 99
percent sure that it's my husband's, but a tiny
part of me worries, because I am a 21-year-old

male and a senior at an Ivy League school, on
the other hand, I am a breeder female and
enjoy great sex with my live-in boy-friend, so
needless to say that I am worried about the
outcome should I tell Selena about my crush,
on the other hand, I'm a 23-year-old bi male
mostly attracted to women, which means that
I'm interested in your thoughts on all of this,
but I am a 23-year-old woman living with my
25-year-old boyfriend, so I'm not a politician,
so I can't give you an answer to that, but I'm a
newly aware bicurious woman newly wed to
the man of my dreams, so needless to say that
I am a 22-year-old college grad who has been
living at home for the last year, because I am
married, and I'm mindful of your rule about
treating younger partners like campsites:
Leave them in better shape than you found
them, and I'm 42 and he's 35, hence I'm 35, gay,
and in a six-year relationship, whereas I'm
torn, and I'm expecting to hear more of that,
thanks to Sewell's book, whereas I am a
39-year-old divorced mother of four, yet I'm a
29-year-old married man, and I am a 21-year-
old single lady and my sex life sucks, also I am
a heterosexual male in my 20s, and I need
some help putting a label on my kink/fetish,

but I'm not saying this particular trucker is a crazed serial killer or an abuser, on the other hand, I am into scat, while I'm a 26-year-old lady who just broke up with a man I thought I wanted to marry, but I'm a straight male in a committed live-in relationship, hence I'm a straight girl who made a resolution to seek out a couple for a three-way, in a word, I'm not worried about STDs because he's been checked, and I'm on the Pill so pregnancy never even enters my mind, and I'm not hideous, but I'm an able-bodied (as of this writing), non-burn-victim (ditto), not-scared-of-my-mommy faggot, what's more, I am currently suffering from loneliness and I need someone to love, yet I am a 22-year-old Chinese male who for the last seven years has been concerned with the size of my penis, also I'm a straight guy, 17-and-a-half, which means that I am rational enough to realize that there is no way that I can pray away these desires, on top of that I'm head over heels for her and for this city, hence I'm a 21-year-old college student living in San Diego, for I am a person who likes to talk about everything, and he is not, so needless to say that I'm going insane, and I don't know if this is a thing, and

research online has not been helpful, also I'm
not super-excited by that idea, on the other
hand, I'm not some hipster who decides his
favorite band is crap the minute the group
hits it big, although I am sure it limits their
income, just as I'm a female in my mid-20s
who loves to give head, and I'm a gay man
who was dating a great guy, hence I am
happily married, but my wife totally despises
my fantasy, and I am a straight, 45-year-old,
monogamous male, just as I am grateful for
what we have together, whereas I am not at all
freaked out by it; I even tried diapering him,
but I am a transgender woman, and I have my
own internalized transphobia that I've had to
navigate around, so I'm about to start my
freshman year in college, and I do not want to
be tied down going into school, whereas I am
a gay male teenager, and I am a new person,
and I feel great, for I'm a 5'9, 300-lbs, but I'm
straight and love being with two men at once
and he's bi so that makes for crazy-hot-fun
times, just as I am a female in my mid-20s,
and I've been openly bi since I was 12, which
means that I am Clio, Euterpe, Thalia, Erato,
Calliope, Urania, Polyhymnia, with a dash of
Jezebel and Venus, although I'm a man in my

early 30s and I've never been in a serious
relationship, but I'm into self-administered
golden showers, so I am ready for the next
phase, and I'm a straight man, age 26, and I'm
the first boy she's ever told about her fetish
and I don't want to disappoint her, just as I
am a 23-year-old lesbian with a beautiful
girlfriend whom I met a month ago, and I'm
way too embarrassed now to ask again,
because it would feel like I was begging him
for fellatio, but I'm a female in a relationship
with a male, hence I am 21 and a virgin, and
I'm a gay 22-year-old male, and my boyfriend
is 24 and seems to have the lowest sex drive
ever, also I'm certain that he hasn't been
unfaithful, but I suspect he's been doing a fair
amount of self-stimulation lately, yet I am a
twentysomething bi guy who loves sucking
cock, and I all but gave your response to
SHEESH a standing ovation, so I'm resenting
this situation more and more, for I'm a
professional Dominatrix in NYC, and I am a
27-year-old male, identify as bisexual, and
enjoy crossdressing—although I have only
crossdressed with guys I meet online, what's
more, I'm dating again after a spate of bad
relationships, for I am a pretty boy, so perhaps

this causes confusion, and I'm a 20-year-old
lesbian, in a word, I'm into chicks, okay, and
I'm a hetero male who has season tickets to
pro football games, and I tailgate before and
after the games, on the other hand, I'm a
24-year-old mostly straight girl with a great
GGG boyfriend, and I am lucky to be with him
in mid-life, because so many of my girlfriends
have unsatisfying sex lives, so I am honest,
hard working, attractive, and fun to be with,
on the other hand, I'm a woman looking for a
Domination/submission thing..., also I'm a
34-year-old straight woman living with a
32-year-old straight man, yet I'm very close to
walking out and taking a break, even though I
believe that marriage is for life, in a word, I'm
a single, straight guy who just turned 30, and
I'm just too damn horny, but I am a 25-year-
old woman and just started dating a great new
guy, and I'm a 20-year-old guy in a long-
distance relationship with my boyfriend of
almost two years, and I'm a straight woman in
my mid-20s living in San Francisco, in a word,
I'm a 27-year-old bisexual chick who just
moved in with my girlfriend of 10 months,
just as I'm an HIV-negative gay guy who ran
an AIDS outreach program for five years in the

1990s, for I am a straight guy, reasonably cute,
who in recent months has begun to attract
women of a much higher caliber than before,
but I'm a 35-year-old divorced man, and I'm a
lesbian, and my friend who is a bi male keeps
asking me to peg him, what's more, I'm a
25-year-old female, which means that I am in
a strange situation, in a word I am 20 years
old and my boyfriend is 30, and I am a gay
man and have had a great friendship with a
guy who had always professed to be straight,
and I am so excited to take this next step, and
so is she, so you can guess that I'm usually the
one spooning up advice to friends hungry for
wisdom, on the other hand, I am a 37-year-
old soccer mom and an avid reader of your
column, which I love—excepting the
santorum stuff, which got tedious, so needless
to say that I'm a 35-year-old straight guy who
works for the post office, which means that I
am a female in my 20s and will soon be
marrying my boyfriend of four years, and I
am dating a girl a bit younger than me, and
we agree on just about everything, although
I'm a 22-year-old straight girl with a lovely
boyfriend of four years, also I'm a happily
married 27-year-old female, so I'm a straight

male in my early 30s and I have a very small
dick, and I'm a 22-year-old female and I lost
my virginity in September 2011, but I had
experienced everything else before that, and
I'm desperate, so I'm talking about bonobos,
also known as pygmy chimpanzees, for I'm
afraid the urine sharing must end, because I
am Smurfette, on top of that I'm avoiding
classes that I don't have friends in because
even if nothing is said (though it often is), the
atmosphere is horrible, on the other hand, I'm
young and I want to experiment while I'm still
energetic and limber, for I am a 31-year-old
straight woman in a monogamous, serious,
two-year relationship, so I'm distraught to the
point of wanting to cheat on him, but I'm
going to feel like an idiot if it's all just a
harmless fantasy, hence I'm a straight male
college student in a relationship, which had
been going great, and I am an attractive
college student, and I'm a fairly athletic guy,
and I got started playing sports partly to
overcome my internal homophobia, hence I'm
sure other folks will have plenty of advice for
the about-to-marry, in a word, I am also a
virgin, and I am a gay male with unusually
large testicles, whereas I'm not turned on by

exercise, nor do I normally notice anyone
sexually appealing during my exercising, yet
I'm not sure what being Mexican has to do
with this issue at all, in a word, I'm thinking
it's much more likely that you would've said
something like My husband is the best, in
addition to that, I am an 18-year-old
pansexual girl, so you can guess that I'm
hoping to take the lead and find out
something about it on my own, although I'm
not turned on by any of that, yet I'm 31, and
you know how many other chances I've had
for a threesome with two attractive,
nonprofessional females, and I'm also not
remotely interested in trying out a first,
although I'm pro-eating pussy the same way
I'm, say, pro-round-the-clock home nursing
for incontinent paraplegics, but I'm not
exactly vanilla, so I'm willing to try pretty
much anything at this point, in a word, I am a
lesbian-identified bi woman who has been
with my ladyfriend (also a LIBW) for seven
years, and I am his first relationship, although
I'm a single, 36-year-old woman, yet I'm a
52-year-old male, divorced, which means that
I'm into bondage and I want a straitjacket, in
addition to that, I'm struggling to understand

the events of the weekend and determine
whether or not I should continue in the
relationship, so I'm guessing SHAG's girlfriend
wouldn't be more forgiving because he
cheated on her with two women, instead of
just one, yet I'm writing regarding Frigid
Frustrated Fool, in addition to that, I'm a
twentysomething female and I've had a fair
number of partners, on top of that I'm a
straight guy, age 22, so needless to say that I'm
also going to give him more orgasms than he
ever thought possible, what's more, I'm a
longtime follower of your column, podcast,
and books, and I hope that someday my son
and I will be as close as you and your mother
were, although I am not sure that this stench
is entirely or at all mine, and I'm just not
interested anymore, on the other hand, I'm
short (five foot two), and most women are
taller than me, yet I'm a straight man who
doesn't get head at home, so needless to say
that I'm thinking—and hoping and praying—
that this letter is complete bullshit, because
I'm a female in my mid 20s, so needless to say
that I'm a gay man in a happy and open
marriage, and I am wet, wet, WET, but I'm a
28-year-old straight guy, also I'm in love,

whereas I am a straight woman who has been
with my fiancé off and on for 12 years, and I'm
in a relationship with a great guy, yet I'm also
a grandmother, hence I'm a straight guy
totally for gay rights in all respects, on the
other hand, I am extremely turned off and
don't know how to tell him that cleanliness is
important to me and the lack of it is killing
our romance, and I am SURE (and my brother
and father agree) that A is gay, like his dad
(long story), in a word, I'm not
complaining—my husband is a wonderful
lover and has been good about taking things
at the right pace for me, and I am and I do, on
the other hand, I'm a straight guy with a great
girlfriend, although I'm a 21-year-old woman
from Canada who sleeps with other women,
which means that I am very much in love
with my male partner, hence I'm a 47-year-old
SBM, and I'm completely serious about this,
which means that I'm a youngish guy having
NSA sex with a friend, and I'm a high-school
student, what's more, I'm not ready for sex,
also I'm among the growing legions of
cuckold fetishists, because I'm into mud and
clay, hence I'm a young gay man, not messed
up, and I ignore people who think there's

something wrong with being gay, so you can guess that I'm a happily married woman in my 30s, but I am very confused by all of this, on the other hand, I am in my 20s, and I'm going to a therapist now, and I'm leaving the s&m collar to my fiancée, whereas I'm extremely dominant—in and out of the bedroom, for I am a 26-year-old hetero male, and I recently started hooking up with a new girl, although I'm not really discriminant [sic] about what girls I date, but I'm getting turned on just thinking about them, and I'm pretty distraught that last night one of my regular chicks saw me do it, whereas I'm a male sub looking for porn videos catering to a femme dom audience, because I'm not having any luck finding a woman interested in having a long-term relationship, just as I'm a 32-year-old heterosexual female who was stricken with near-terminal cancer eight years ago, so I am a mature teenage girl with a question for you, for I'm writing because I am at a loss for what to do, so needless to say that I'm not looking for yet another video of penis torture and/or anal rape, where the female dom inevitably gives her slave a blowjob, which means that I'm not trying to be a party

crasher, Dan, I'm just looking to keep DOM
out of trouble, yet I am left this morning with
confusion and trepidation about my
relationship with my new girlfriend, so I'm
not black, but I am not white, so needless to
say that I'm leaving, just as I'm not saying that
he's a creep or an abuser—or that he's not,
and I'm a 32-year-old single heterosexual
female, also I'm at wits' end with this, in
addition to that, I am a 25-year-old straight
woman who recently got out of a
monogamous relationship, and I'm also
concerned about this being bad for me in the
long run, like how the death grip is for guys,
although I'm extremely idealistic, and I count
myself as a romantic, in addition to that, I'm
in love with her and I want to spend the rest
of my life with her, on top of that I'm
attractive, but the boys I know have
concluded that I am crazy because of my
recent history, on the other hand, I am in
desperate need, although I'm sure this
question is way too boring for your column,
whereas I'm receiving treatment, but I'm still
not ever clean enough to bottom confidently,
and I'm trying to put my finger on why it
bothers me—I mean, if I'm okay with him

looking at it, I shouldn't be aghast when I see
it, right, so I'm another statistic in America's
march towards obesity, on the other hand, I'm
only paying her to tie me up and step on me,
in a word, I'm just in denial about it—lifelong,
everlasting denial, with any luck, although I'm
going to see my Aunt Peg at my brother's
wedding this July, at which time she will no
doubt peg the shit out of me for doing this to
her, in addition to that, I'm a gay high-school
junior and I'm dying for the advice people
wished they had when they were my age, so
I'm not going to do that to anyone again, just
as I'm now thrilled to have a new boyfriend
who is GGG and as kinky as I am, so you can
guess that I'm now concerned about how
much a set of balls counts in the gay
community, for I'm in the Pacific Northwest,
if that makes a difference, but I'm a single
straight guy who really enjoys performing oral
sex on women, yet I'm a bi woman, he's a
straight man, and I'm pretty open-minded but
I don't want to put us at risk for an STD, nor
do I understand why he would want to share
me with some stranger, yet I'm a loyal fan and
a physician who cares for people living with
HIV, just as I'm surprised that you let UNCLE

off so easy, because I'm in my mid-30s and
not sure what I should do, what's more, I am
with a girl who is a female ejaculator, on top
of that I'm writing to help out the lovely lady
who wrote in asking how she could meet
skater-boys, because I'm a 20-year-old girl,
and I've been dating my boyfriend, who is 23,
for two years, and I'm just terrified he's going
to harm someone, in a word, I am not
complaining, but I'm thinking of going and
telling his wife, yet I'm a 31-year-old gay man,
so I am 14 years old and I live in South East
London, and I'm tired and frustrated and
hurt, which means that I am at this time more
comfortable without the nervousness of an
emotional entanglement—so please don't tell
me to just find a nice guy, what's more, I'm in
love with Trent Ford, because I'm old enough
now, but could I just say I was over 18 the
whole time they were being made, yet I'm a
26-year-old straight female, also I'm afraid
that if she finds out, she'll drop out of school
in shame, so needless to say that I'm not even
sure that fake pregnant equals fake fat, but
that is beside the point, which means that I
am now over my feelings for her, and a few
months ago we began talking again, although

I'm a bi-ish college girl and used to be in a sexually unsatisfying long-distance relationship, in a word, I'm a 19-year-old lesbian with the dyke equivalent of the does size matter problem: I have a really short tongue, which means that I'm pro-porn and I'm pro-porn-cam girls, and I'm not trying to insult people who save themselves for marriage, for I am dating a divorcée who just turned 60, which means that I am a transgender gurl living in the heart of South Beach, Florida, just as I'm sounding like a prude and a killjoy, for I'm 15 and have no experience with this stuff, so I'm 26, bi, female, and my idea of a successful long-term relationship lands somewhere between monogamish—awesome word—and completely nonmonogamous, what's more, I am a girl and I am stuck, hence I'm going to take it back, on the other hand, I'm a 28-year-old straight guy, which means that I am assuming that what he meant here is that if you are experiencing pain during anal sex, you probably shouldn't proceed, so I'm still with the same woman and I'm no longer suicidal over my internalized homophobia, and I'm also coming out of a five-year relationship, for

I'm afraid to ask him to use this numbing
cream I saw while at a sex-toy party, on top of
that I am all for cunnilingus, and I'm seeing
an amazing guy who I met doing sex work—
as in, he was paying me for straight-up sex,
yet I'm a 21-year-old woman with bi-curious
tendencies who's been in a committed
relationship for four years, although I'm a
straight guy, and if I met a woman online, I
would want to be sure she had female
genitalia under her clothes, just as I am
starting to be turned off by this, and I don't
see her as desirable anymore, but I'm male,
primarily hetero, and my wife and I are in our
early 40s, in a word, I am not a virgin, but
every romantic relationship I've tried to
pursue has ended in disaster, for I'm 30 and
enjoy women between the ages of 35 and 45,
but can't seem to find a place in Edmonton to
meet them, also I am not looking for a
monogamous relationship, just a mutually
respectful fling, although I'm 42 years old and
I've been involuntarily celibate for TEN years,
and I'm trying to think about other things,
pleasant things, so needless to say that I'm not
going to ask you the usual straight-girl
question, and I am desperately seeking

Cheryl, because I'm herpes-free, but I found
out today that my roommate has contracted
it, so I'm a 24-year-old straight male, which
means that I'm a lesbian, and I'd sworn never
to date a bisexual woman, and I'm 25 and have
been with my 27-year-old boyfriend for five
years, in a word, I'm hoping to stay under
$100, also I'm a man, also I am a 25-year-old
bi female with a bi male partner, and I am
happily married to a girl in her mid-20s, so
needless to say that I'm a bisexual man,
although I'm a 21-year-old college student,
whereas I'm not 100 percent comfortable
sharing the ladies' room with him, and I'm an
18-year-old, closeted, bisexual high-school
student, just as I'm totally fucking weirded
out by that, and I'm grappling with three
issues: (1) Did she cheat, although I'm only 22,
for God's sake, for I am a straight female and
I've been in a relationship for two years, so I
am a few years from 40, and I'm a gay male
and have been seeing a terrific guy for a couple
of months, in a word, I'm pretty sure you've
told us this before, Dan, but I think this guy
needs a reminder, on the other hand, I'm
writing on behalf of a 19-year-old guy with
cerebral palsy, because I'm actually having a

hard time connecting with him, just as I am a
23-year-old straight male, yet I'm an 18-year-
old girl in my freshman year at university,
what's more, I'm a straight college guy, age 21,
and I share a house with some buddies and a
couple, so needless to say that I'm also a boy,
age 15, and I hadn't gotten around to coming
out to my parents yet, and I'm wondering
how someone with my kinks should approach
dating, whereas I am a woman who is into
commitment, loyalty, love, trust, and honesty,
for I'm not so into it, and I'm a 19-year-old
gay guy in a relationship with an 18-year-old
gay guy (for nearly four years), on the other
hand, I am still in love with my ex, also I'm
sure they would be happy to go all the way if
they found a willing participant, in addition
to that, I'm not out to my mom, so I'm not a
lesbian, and I'm a 23-year-old gay dude from
Vancouver, just as I am a 28-year-old woman
living in a town with a big military base, and
I'm going bonkers because my husband is
impotent, hence I'm terrified of that guy, to
tell you the truth, and I am a 21-year-old gay
male and I finally met a man I'm interested in,
for I am in college and in a super-fantastic
relationship, just as I'm a dom and she's a

switch in our part-time BDSM relationship,
but I'm having problems separating my desire
to be humiliated sexually from a willingness
to be humiliated socially, and I am an 18-year-
old British queer girl who was recently
involved with an older woman while visiting
the United States, because I'm a 15-year-old
male in need of advice, in a word, I am quite
certain he would be outraged about such a
revelation, so I'm inclined to say nothing, on
top of that I am writing to correct one of the
replies you gave in Pussypalooza '99, hence
I'm almost five feet tall, and weigh 108 lbs,
what's more, I am 32 years old and married to
my best friend who wants nothing to do with
me sexually, but I am a single, sexually active
woman in my early 40s, and I am so worried,
in addition to that, I am a very young,
attractive girl, although I'm a 20-year-old bi
guy and a very attractive dude, on the other
hand, I'm a 27-year-old divorced woman,
which means that I'm into ball busting—
getting slapped or kicked in the nuts—but my
wife was never willing, also I am enjoying the
heightened sexual arousal, and my GGG
girlfriend is thrilled, and I am trying my best
to roll with it and become more comfortable

with myself, but it is a struggle, so I'm a
middle-aged guy, so needless to say that I'm
glad it happens, I just don't want to do it, so
I'm glad I caught him in bed with another
man before I married him and not after, on
the other hand, I'm a bisexual woman
married to a wonderful man, and I am not
certain about all the dynamics at play here, so
I'm stumped, Dan, for I'm mainly interested
in being serviced orally but have yet to fulfill
this longing, and I'm a transsexual man
(formerly a woman), and can identify because
I have no dick, on the other hand, I am a
woman who has been with my male partner
for one year, in addition to that, I'm 21 and
still a virgin, and I'm going to make this
marriage work, although I'm submissive and
masochistic; he's dominant and willing to
inflict some pain, on top of that I'm not
asking to have sex when I'm on my heavy
days, just at the beginning and tail end of my
period, whereas I'm now 39 and still a virgin,
and I'm just another voice out there telling
women there's something wrong with them if
they don't cater to a man's every whim, in
addition to that, I am a 22-year-old
heterosexual female, in a word, I'm also into

other minor scarring, as well, and I'm scared
of him and turned on by him, what's more,
I'm not sure he even knows he does it, which
means that I am horny, steamy, and sexy
straight male in my late 20s, for I'm a gay
Roman Catholic, in addition to that, I am
disgusted with the person I am and feel so
dirty, because I'm her first boyfriend, and I'm
getting married in a few months, and I
wouldn't be so blissfully in love if it weren't for
your advice, because I'm a 23-year-old male
who has never been in a relationship, which
means that I'm not into public sex or group
sex; that's just not appealing to me, also I am a
woman in a relatively new relationship, and
I'm finding myself obsessing over him (like I
said, he is fine), but the more I do, the more
pathetic I feel, so I'm also lying and cheating,
because I'm a straight man married to a
bisexual lady, which is something I would
recommend to all other straight men in the
world, also I am not down with sharing her,
but I am willing to do it because otherwise
some other girl will do it for her, in a word,
I'm a 23-year-old gay male who was diagnosed
four years ago with ADHD, yet I'm sorry this
desire of mine has caused so much pain in our

relationship, in addition to that, I'm a bi male in a long-distance, long-term, and hypothetically poly relationship, and I'm going to a speed-dating event soon, although I'm a 16-year-old girl whose 20-year-old brother has a foot fetish, what's more, I'm a gay man and a hunter; he's a gay boy and a vegan, in a word, I'm as pro-cunnilingus as a gay man can get, but I guess you could say I'm pro-cunnilingus in the abstract, what's more, I'm a 24-year-old female and I've been with my boyfriend for five years, and I am a straight 19-year-old girl in college, hence I'm now 30, straight, and married, and I am a straight, 18-year-old girl and a college freshman, so I am a freshman in college and a virgin, so needless to say that I'm 45, female, and married to a smart, funny, intelligent 50-year-old man, on the other hand, I'm a polyamorous bisexual college student whose parents already think I'm a slut, and I'm not sure if this should be a deal breaker or if this is just a disagreement, and I am physically fit, and although I'm not a beauty, I'm pretty enough, for I'm a young, attractive straight female, what's more, I'm a mostly gay male with a boyfriend who is also mostly gay, and

I'm a 30-year-old male, my boss is a few years
younger and female, and she's generally cool,
for I'm a 33-year-old man, married eight years
and mostly happy, and I am a 28-year-old
woman who has been with my boyfriend for
two years, also I'm a straight guy, so needless
to say that I am in love with her, although I
am very disturbed because I am actually
aroused by content that shows supposedly
straight men degrading gay men, and I am 52
years old, and this condition has gotten worse
as I have gotten older, which means that I'm a
28-year-old gay guy living happily with my
boyfriend, and I'm sure there has to be an
HIV-positive social/support group in Toronto,
so needless to say that I'm having a problem,
on top of that I'm not sure I want to work
that hard, particularly in August, and I am
attracted to him, in a word, I'm having an
argument with a friend, and I'm ashamed of
not being able to accommodate my guy
without the help of saliva, Astroglide, or
Vaseline, in addition to that, I am a black gay
male and live in Portland, Oregon, and I'm
also very involved with the Episcopal Church
and want to become a leader in my church, on
the other hand, I'm not worried about being

hit on, but I feel like hanging out at a gay club would be somewhat dishonest and touristy, whereas I am ass over teakettle in love with a boy, so I'm 28 and have had a disability since birth, for I am a GGG girlfriend, and I'm up for pretty much anything my boyfriend wants to do, because I am a natural sub, but my girlfriend asked to switch and for me to dominate her, for I am a weekly reader of your column, so you can guess that I am a 21-year-old male in a two-year relationship with a 20-year-old girl, just as I'm a 23-year-old straight boy from Italy, and my problem is a friend and his girlfriend, yet I'm the creative type: I write, I draw, I compose, also I'm a 46-year-old male who has a thing for younger women, on top of that I'm a straight, vanilla 29-year-old woman, happily married to a kinky bi guy for six years, together for 13, yet I am currently typing one-handed because I am shoving my fist deep into my lower back as some sort of half-assed pressure-point massage, on the other hand, I'm a straight 36-year-old guy, for I am a 20-year-old male, and as such have certain desires that almost all 20-year-old males have (desires of a sexual nature), and I'm a nice girl from Nashville

who moved to New York and met a sweet-as-
pie guy, what's more, I'm a hetero male in my
late 30s, and this incident took place over a
decade ago, but I've felt guilty about it ever
since, yet I'm going to see him again, and I
don't think I'll be able to make the same
excuse again, so I'm sorry, but that's just sick,
and I'm a 23-year-old homo who came out
one year ago, on top of that I'm one of those
women who loves to see a man get busy with
another man, and I am your typical straight
Joe, yet I am fairly picky, but I meet many
women I am attracted to, in a word, I am a
straight female and have been in a loving
relationship with my boyfriend for three
years, and I am a 19-year-old straight male
who is only attracted to chubby girls, though I
myself am rather skinny, so needless to say
that I'm 23 and confused, although I'm an
18-year-old girl whose 19-year-old boyfriend
gets off on domination, and I'm a 26-year-old
straight girl and I've been dating this great guy
for a few months, and I'm calling because I
care about your health, what's more, I'm a
senior in college and a lesbian, and I have a
question about strap-on etiquette, in addition
to that, I am 29 and attractive, although I am a

25-year-old straight woman, in a word, I'm
into BDSM and my safe word is safe word, and
I'm a 34-year-old guy with a kink that my last
boyfriend indulged to the limit, although I'm
a 53-year-old woman, so you can guess that I
am morbidly obese and have been for most of
my life, for I'm a straight female in her early
20s, currently engaged to a handsome man
three years older, so needless to say that I'm a
straight black guy in love with Asian women,
and I'm happy with my current girlfriend—I
love her—but these panties really turn me on,
but I'm 16, female, and Australian, and I
identify as bi (out to friends, not parents),
although I'm a 32-year-old woman with two
young kids, married five years, and I am really
scared that he will find that I am inept at sex,
hence I am an 18-year-old straight girl, and
I'm never going to tell him that I got knocked
up on purpose, yet I'm happy for him if it's
what he truly wants, but I feel like he did it
out of desperation, what's more, I'm not
talking about a little embarrassment, Dan,
but lasting trauma, since I am a 22-year-old
female and I've been with my 21-year-old
boyfriend for two years, also I'm a straight
18-year-old girl in my first sexual relationship,

on the other hand, I'm not sure that I ever
will be, whereas I'm really ashamed of my
feelings because I do love kids, hence I'm a
26-year-old FTM who is interested in seeing
what sex with gay men is like, which means
that I'm a mostly hetero male who's recently
been hit upon by a gay male and I don't know
how to respond, also I'm a male with
submissive tendencies, and my wife decides
when I get to orgasm, which means that I'm
wondering now whether this is something I
need to get off, in addition to that, I'm looking
for some real advice, for I'm not attracted to
heavy men and I have never slept with an
overweight man, which means that I'm really
not sure how I feel about this, but I am
definitely feeling something, also I'm tired of
fouling things up and making myself lonely,
but I am a 19-year-old university student, just
as I'm a 27-year-old bi girl, so you can guess
that I'm a 19-year-old gay male, also I'm a guy
who gets off on dirty panties, which means
that I'm 100 percent monogamous, but a toy
is a toy is a toy, hence I'm a 20-year-old gay
male and I entered into a relationship with a
guy at the beginning of the summer, and I am
a straight woman who likes getting fucked in

the ass, and I am a straight, monogamous man with normal sexual predilections, in a word, I'm a single (mostly) gay guy who is curious about women, for I am a straight, crossdressing male into bondage, on top of that I'm honest: We got divorced because I cheated on my wife, so you can guess that I'm assuming you're running Windows and what I recommend here is virtualization software, so I'm deeply torn, on the other hand, I'm not attracted to him—in fact, the thought of kissing another guy repulses me; forget about anal sex, and I'm wondering if I should say anything to him, whereas I am a 20-year-old straight female dating the boy of my dreams, so I am in love with an intelligent woman, on the other hand, I'm not super-pleased about ruining my mattress, and the postcoital sleeping on very wet sheets is not ideal, so I'm a former smoker myself who has worked with cancer patients, so needless to say that I'm working with Wikipedia, where we're currently debating the Donkey Punch, hence I am a 58-year-old gay man, yet I'm pretty GGG, Dan, but this is one thing where I draw the line, because I'm into farts, although I am an avid reader of your column in Edmonton,

Alberta, so you can guess that I'm a straight
female, overweight, but it's in all the right
places, and I'm 26 now and I've been into feet
pretty much since I was 8 years old, yet I am a
27-year-old female with an active sex life, in a
word, I am in a monogamous relationship, so
I am not concerned at the moment about
STDS, in addition to that, I'm 18 years old and
my girlfriend and I have been engaging in
sexual acts, so needless to say that I'm not
sure if this is funny or horrible, but the other
day, she was strapped to the bed and just as
she was reaching a climax, I stopped, and I'm
21 and my girlfriend is 22, in a word, I am
emotionally and financially drained, and I'm
not sure I can do that, either, although I'm not
talking about porn directed by men for
submissive men, but porn targeting the
appetites of the dominatrix, which means that
I'm convinced a swinging scene exists here,
but I have no idea how to find it, for I'm not
bad-looking, so you can guess that I'm getting
mixed advice from different people and I just
want a straight answer, and I'm voting for
Ralph Nader, and I'm convinced that he's too
good for me, also I am a lesbian and broke up
a year ago with my girlfriend of four years, on

the other hand, I am, too, but having had
girlfriends makes me comfortable knowing
that I mostly want to be with men, and I am a
20-year-old woman going to school in New
York, what's more, I'm not on anyone's side in
this dispute, yet I'm a 24-year-old female, I've
been with my boyfriend for four years, and
the sex is just…, and I am a heterosexual guy,
married, yet I am cheerful, good-humored,
and pretty, too, on the other hand, I'm
thinking a parent can't let that go as easily, yet
I am completely satisfied, hence I am so
depressed by this situation, whereas I'm a
23-year-old het male, and I am married, so I'm
above average in terms of looks (I work out)
and I'm pretty smart (I went to a top school),
in a word, I'm a hetero college female and my
boyfriend and I are sexually active, which
means that I am worried, though, that my son
will get hurt, also I'm a straight guy, and my
girlfriend just read my journal, also I am a
very single, 41-year-old, African American
butch lesbian who does not smoke cigarettes,
drink alcohol, nor use drugs, for I'm
completely heterosexual, too, yet I'm a
23-year-old male who is bi-curious/pan-
curious/post-gender-curious, but I'm so

confused on what to do, and I'm starting to
think I'm broken; the last few years, I've felt
pretty cut off from my sexuality, on top of
that I'm a 25-year-old gay male into puppy
play, and I'm a longtime reader (I'm sure
you're thrilled), so I know my interests aren't
on your approved list of sexual activities,
because I am a married 54-year-old
postmenopausal woman, in addition to that, I
am intelligent, blonde, I have a good figure,
but ALL the guys I've been with lately have
dumped me, and I'm sure you can see where
this is leading: My dick is really small, yet I'm
a straight woman in her late 20s dating the
one, by which I mean the man who I'd be
happy to wind up married to, and I am a
recently married 30-year-old straight guy, yet I
am a 16-year-old straight male—I think, so I
am also a stubborn motherfucker, also I'm a
decent-looking guy, just never got laid, not
even a blowjob—hell, I have practically no
sexual experience, in a word, I am a 36-year-
old straight man, blissfully married to my
34-year-old soul mate, on top of that I'm just
wondering if there's anything I can do to help
her get rid of the demons of the past, and I
am a 21-year-old woman, on the other hand,

I'm a single gay male in my late 20s, so I'm
crazy about her and we're taking things slow,
but I am a straight woman—AND I LOVE
GIVING HEAD, what's more, I am a completely
straight guy, and I'm an 18-year-old female,
and I'm speaking from experience—how
about you, on the other hand, I'm a 23-year-
old, single gay man, also I'm sure your readers
have been following the gay marriage hoopla
in Massachusetts and San Francisco, in a
word, I am a young female currently in a
relationship and I want to be honest with my
boyfriend, on top of that I'm a 25-year-old
male, and I'm uncut and the head of my cock
was really sensitive, just like UNCUT, but my
problem wasn't premature ejaculation,
although I'm a college athlete who recently
got a strange offer from a former TA, and I'm a
32-year-old male; my girlfriend is 39, and I'm
fine with this, but we work different
schedules, so it's not realistic, although I am
almost getting obsessed myself, checking the
sites and his chats constantly, and I am
curious about what to do when the time
comes, in addition to that, I'm an 18-year-old
straight male and a virgin, because I'm with a
great guy, and our sex life is awesome, and I

am a 34-year-old straight, single female, in
addition to that, I'm going to a university
about 3,000 miles away next fall, on the other
hand, I'm a 28-year-old black male, living in
Toronto, and I am starting to wonder about
going on some method of birth control, what's
more, I'm a 23-year-old guy and I have been
dating my 21-year-old girlfriend for two years,
and I'm considering having a threesome with
a couple, but the friend I routinely confide in
about my sexual adventures has warned me
against it, so I'm a married straight man, and I
am marrying a man with two children—a boy
and a girl—and we want to include his
children in our wedding party, but I'm
uncomfortable with the idea of him going
over to play with these men without me there,
but I find these bondage sessions really
tedious, on top of that I'm not related to any
of the contestants, so you can feel free to send
me to Vegas with someone who looks really
good in his TWS, also I'm a pretty sexual
person, I masturbate regularly, and I have a
good sexual imagination, which means that
I'm sure you can see this coming: After we got
married and had a child, my wife changed her
mind about the threesome, hence I'm so tired

in the morning, and my mom blames me saying I stay up too late, so needless to say that I am a man who has been in an open marriage for 10 years, although I'm a young man, in the prime of my life, living in the youth capital of the world, San Francisco, so I'm not sure if this has anything to do with the desire I feel for my mother, on the other hand, I'm a 24-year-old gay man who is a little traumatized, on top of that I'm a bi, crip woman in my 40s who's had plenty of wild, wacky sex throughout the years without paying, just as I am paranoid that security is going to confront me, so needless to say that I'm a gay male, and I have a thing for crossdressers, but I am a straight guy who's curious about men, so I am very familiar with one kink: diapers, because I'm just concerned that they're gonna be a little pissed off, and I am a 20-year-old male who has a fetish that other people just don't understand, so you can guess that I'm a 20-year-old straight male, but this isn't really about me, because I'm a 24-year-old male and I lost my virginity to my girlfriend last year, what's more, I am worried about how she would get along financially without me, and I'm a gay man with HIV, on

top of that I'm afraid we're reaching an
impasse on this issue, on the other hand, I'm a
28-year-old woman, and I'm a gay man who
gained 30 pounds after I met my current
boyfriend, for I'm not sure why they're
suddenly marketing hot-and-cool lubes to
breeders so aggressively, also I'm referring to
your reply to Montana Momma's letter and
your comment, one of the main features of
homosexuality is promiscuity, what's more, I
am only 24 years old and I needed to explore
other fish in the sea, just as I am delighted to
have the chance to e-mail my heartaches, so I
am open minded sexually, and I understand
that looking at feet is an unstoppable urge for
him, for I'm level-headed, direct, and ALWAYS
honest, even when it hurts, and I'm baby-
stepping my way toward an offline search for
guys, going to events hosted by the local gay
pride center, so I'm certainly into love, and I'm
a straight 20-year-old woman in a relationship
with a straight 30-year-old male, and I'm a
21-year-old bi guy, because I was recently
hanging out at my university's Queer
Collective when the issue of the F word came
up, on the other hand, I am an attractive,
normal 24-year-old female who enjoys taking

pictures of myself nude for my own personal
use, just as I'm thinking silk, and I'm very
respectful outside the bedroom: I buy her
flowers, I write to her when she's away, and I
make sure to treat her friends well, on the
other hand, I'm losing my hair, growing love
handles, I've only got a teacher's salary—not
exactly a catch, also I am a 29-year-old gay
male, and I have a problem, in a word, I'm
longing to spawn, so I've decided to get
pregnant and not tell him, what's more, I am
afraid that telling him would offend him and
that he will stop doing it, in addition to that,
I'm a muscular 42-year-old man and I have
some body hair and I've been told that I look
fucking hot in briefs, but I am about to marry
a caring and intelligent man, an amazing lover,
a total stud, beyond well endowed, someone
who gets me, so you can guess that I'm still
good friends with one furry guy I met
through my ex-roommate, and I'm 25, I live in
Portland, and my boyfriend and I have been
monogamous for five years, just as I am a bit
of a sadist myself, and some of my friends are
sadists, for I am a straight teen boy who's
addicted to masturbating, but I'm not going
to let this happen to me again because I never

want to feel this way again, although I'm a 25-year-old girl dating a 26-year-old guy, and I am writing to you regarding the letter from Wanting Time For Myself, the young man being abused by his emotionally needy girlfriend, on top of that I am begging for any kind of advice you can give because right now I am screwed up in the head, just as I am happy to do lighter stuff, but I am a 24-year-old gay man living in a major urban center, what's more, I am not interested in squeezing into an able corset and using a flogger on him, in a word, I'm an 18-year-old girl, going off to college, and I'm not sure how to identify myself, yet I'm a 34-year-old woman who needs a vibrator to get off, and for years I felt defective, on the other hand, I'm dead certain if he's used my insertables, that he did so without putting condoms on them first, and I'm still debating whether to send it or not for fear that the whole family might find out, so I am 27, and my wife, ,Marybeth,' is 26, on top of that I'm interested in meeting her, if you can hook us up, because I'm a 26-year-old girl, and my boyfriend is bi, so I am a lesbian, completely sexually satisfied when I have sex with women and never sexually satisfied when

I have sex with men, so needless to say that
I'm a 28-year-old, professional, single woman,
and I'm a straight woman, 23 years old, and I
am in my mid-20s, and while I flirt with
poverty, I have a respectable and comfortable
one-bedroom apartment, on the other hand,
I'm not bothered by that either, yet I'm very
curious about sex and I want to lose my
virginity, but I'm not even into men, in
addition to that, I am writing to you to
apologize for the tons of whiny complaints
from my fellow straight women, and I'm not
being glib, but I'm a 34-year-old male, and 99
percent of my relationships (sexual and not)
have been with women two to 20 years my
senior, which means that I'm not comfortable
with your motives, for I'm a straight woman,
Dan, with an amazing boyfriend who I fuck
all the time, but I'm just curious whether or
not he's right, hence I'm suddenly married to
a NUN, and I am a 23-year-old female devotee
of disabled men, on the other hand, I am a
19-year-old woman in my first serious
relationship, although I'm a guy, and the
couple in question is M/F, also I am a 24-year-
old female, in a word, I'm afraid to reveal this
to anyone, on the other hand, I'm a virgin,

and I am hoping you can possibly give me
some perspective, so needless to say that I'm a
hustler myself, and I always use condoms
when I suck guys off, for I'm female, and I've
known that I am bisexual for all my adult life,
what's more, I am a very sexual person, and
she kept me satisfied with oral, dress-up, sex
in different places—things like that, just as
I'm dating the man of my dreams, and I am a
het woman engaged to be married to a man I
love very deeply, and I'm a female college
senior and I'm going to graduate in a couple
of months, so you can guess that I'm deep,
what's more, I am a 17-year-old girl growing
up in an adoptive family in Australia, yet I'm
being GGG, and she absolutely gets off on it, in
addition to that, I am a 19-year-old male with
a 4.5-inch cock that has not grown since I was
12, and I am prepared now to be the boyfriend
that she wanted me to be, yet I'm 35 years old,
attractive, and trying to date, whereas I'm a
19-year-old FTM who identifies as queer, on
top of that I am just so terrified of being
dismissed as a potential partner because of
the way we met, for I'm 19 years old, and for a
while I was looking at disgusting stuff online
to see if I blanched at it, for I'm a 31-year-old

white gay man, although I'm 50 years old now, and I still think about boys, so needless to say that I'm in decent shape, but I would need to cut out beer and chocolate to achieve any sort of show-offable stomach, which means that I am so totally not gay, because I'm a straight male and I love my fiancée, what's more, I'm horribly embarrassed, just as I am a 28-year-old female graduate student, and I am really a female, although I'm a 19-year-old bisexual student at an all-girl college which is seemingly chock full of lesbians/bi girls, and I am living with a gay man who I used to have a crush on, and we would both do anything for each other in bed, but I am a 31-year-old gay male and have been with my 27-year-old boyfriend for a year, although I'm not saying bi guys are bad people, or they don't make great one-night stands, but I'm 35 and she's 20, in a word, I'm a virgin, so needless to say that I am feeling conflicted, in addition to that, I'm a 30-year-old straight male who fell in love with a girl who didn't want to proceed with a relationship, but I am an available sexual outlet, for I am an 18-year-old girl with an 18-year-old guy, although I'm the woman who had that boy tied up in my bedroom

during a party this summer, and I am so glad
that I trusted my instincts instead of doing
what was proper, hence I'm under no illusion
that I'm what he's looking for, on the other
hand, I'm now convinced that women are
almost exclusively attracted to COMPLETE
FUCKING CREEPS, and I'm having a problem,
however, finding sites with fresh, free stuff
that will actually play streaming on the
iPhone, for I'm a 30ish woman in a lovely GGG
relationship with a man about my age, so I am
all for cunnilingus, and I'm sorry if that's
harsh, but that's the way it is, in addition to
that, I am a gay man who has been in a
relationship with my partner for nine years,
and I'm embarrassed, my feelings are hurt,
and I'm annoyed, because I am a sex-crazed
woman, yet I am dying to say to her, I am
super-attracted to you and I don't want to
assume anything about your agreements with
your hubby, what's more, I'm the girl the
straight men go to after their female
girlfriends go home, and I'm not sure what to
do about this, so needless to say that I'm a
mostly heterosexual woman in my mid-30s in
a very vanilla relationship with my husband
for the past 14 years, although I'm turned on

by the idea of a dominant guy, but most of the
guys I attract are pure vanilla, and I'm a
happily married woman, in a word, I'm a guy
into she-male porn, and I've noticed that
almost all the models in said porn have very
tight scrotums, which means that I'm a male
in my early 20s, in a word, I'm also doing well
in the sex and self-respect departments,
thanks, and I am a 25-year-old straight male,
and I'm a straight male, 21 years old, hence I'm
into bondage, and like looking at pictures of
tied-up and gagged girls on the Internet and
jerking off to them, also I'm a 27-year-old gay
man who is only attracted to straight men,
and I'm a college freshman, but I'm not going
to be here long enough to look for an LTR, just
as I'm no toothpick either, at 5'11, 330 pounds,
so she won't let me get on top of her, although
I am currently trying to examine my morals
to see if I can be okay with this arrangement,
which means that I am a 23-year-old male
who has been in a relationship with a great
woman for four years now, yet I'm not so sure,
on the other hand, I am 54 and divorced
twice, so I am a man who tends to ejaculate
prematurely, in addition to that, I'm dating a
boy back in the US who I absolutely adore,

but we're not necessarily exclusive, on the other hand, I'm a little put off because he was the one who pushed for exclusivity and the title of boyfriend, because I'm a 23-year-old straight female, on top of that I'm a 21-year-old straight guy with a boring sex life, what's more, I am writing about a friend, but I am a straight 36-year-old, and I have bad breath, and I am ashamed because it seems pretty perverse and disturbed, so I am a woman in my 20s, although I am a pretty experienced girl who settled down with a sweet, attentive, funny, wonderful guy, and I am a straight female who was a dominatrix for a while-and out of all the jobs I've had, I loved it the most, so needless to say that I am turned on by the idea of someone eating a lot of food, usually junk food, and putting on weight, for I'm the first person to admit that I don't understand all this, and I'm a 23-year-old gay guy, yet I'm now having a hard time finding people willing to have casual-yet-kinky sex, although I'm a 40-year-old vegetarian guy living in a small college town and looking for an LTR, and I'm getting one or two calls or texts per week meant for this other woman, which means that I am a 45-year-old married male and I'm

into enemas, in addition to that, I am totally
capable of getting over one drunken kiss—
everybody makes mistakes, just as I am a
college student just trying to get through my
senior year with some halfway decent grades
and a smidge of sanity, in addition to that, I
am a gay man and have been in a relationship
with my GGG boyfriend for more than three
years, in a word, I'm also five feet six and 124
pounds, and I'm married to a woman I love,
but our sex life has become unbearable, for
I'm a white 31-year-old man in Ohio planning
a move to Washington, D.C, so I'm a 17-year-
old girl, and I've only had one boyfriend—
who was, at the time, 21 and, I thought,
perfect, yet I'm afraid that if he finds
someone, my jealousy—which I work very
hard to hide from him—will break us up, on
top of that I'm afraid that he will refuse to see
the obvious, and in turn resent me for being
the bearer of bad news, in addition to that,
I'm glad you decided to drop the Hey, Faggot
salutation, which I've always hated, so
needless to say that I'm also not too deeply
involved with that community, so maybe I
just don't see the activism happening, on the
other hand, I'm 38 and have no boyfriend or

friends to go out with, and I'm writing to
complain about your thoughtless reply to
Mama Violates Poppa, although I am a
female, yet I'm a 24-year-old straight girl, and
vaginal sex does nothing for me, what's more,
I'm a bi girl, and I am a longtime reader of
your column, hence I'm willing to bet that, as
twentysomethings living in New York City,
they engaged in the consumption of alcohol
and possibly other substances, and I'm angry
that the lack of frequent sex is what drove
him to porn, but now the problem is that I
want it too much, so I am a 24-year-old
lesbian who has been out for five years, and I
am a teenage boy with a strange attraction to
bestiality, although I'm a single man in my 30s
who loves to throw up on my partner during
sex, and I love it even more when she (my
partner) throws up on me, so I'm interested in
an intense and consuming love affair with a
woman, which means that I'm dying to find
out more about tranny scrotums, female
pastors, selective semen allergies, clit Tabasco,
for I'm 47 and have three kids, and I am a
genetic male with questions about my gender
identity, although I am a mid-20s woman
relatively new to masturbating, in a word, I'm

still fertile but don't want to end up pregnant
by one of our thirds, so we're taking every
conceivable precaution, because I am also
married, yet I'm on vacation and currently in
something of an impaired-state holding
pattern over the Pacific Ocean, on the other
hand, I am a 21-year-old student who, after
reading last week's column, has a proposition
for the loser who wants to be farted on,
because I am actually quite into the idea, but I
was shocked to learn that he intends to have a
threesome whether or not it's with me,
because I'm a 27-year-old lesbian, and my
girlfriend of two years broke up with me, for
I'm still friendly with my ex, although I have
tremendous guilt issues over not having
figured myself out before dragging him into a
marriage, so I'm talking gentle, external
stroking with lubed-up fingers, lots of licking,
vibrators placed on your butthole (that's on,
or across, not in), and I am a 30-year-old
woman, so you can guess that I'm poly, just as
I'm a 21-year-old, in a word, I am too
ashamed to ask a single soul in the world
these questions, in addition to that, I'm
thinking the wife misses her boobs too,
although I'm a straight guy and I'm really into

having my balls sucked—it's one of my
favorite things and just thinking about it
turns me on, so needless to say that I am a
60-year-old man who recently lost his wife to
cancer, in addition to that, I'm a gay man of
about 30, in a relationship with a great guy,
and I am a heterosexual female, and I'm an
ex-lesbian, so I thought I might as well share
my experiences and theories with you,
because I am a tall Asian guy, six foot one, 165
pounds, cut and lean, 32 but look 28, and I'm
not going to say it can't be exciting or a
turn-on, but I'm a straight girl who started
dating this straight guy six months ago, so
needless to say that I'm a 30-year-old gay guy
and moved from one city to another, whereas
I am amazed and envious of men who say
they have had to go without sex for only a
month, on top of that I'm a healthy, sexually
active college student in Wisconsin, and I'm a
19-year-old guy with a big problem, because I
am a 26-year-old female, and I've been with
my boyfriend for almost five years, and I'm
GGG, he probably gets more blowjobs than
most married men, and I love having sex with
him, on the other hand, I'm new to all of this
parenting stuff, but I know that he can't

continue to see this person, and I am not
trying to make him feel bad or put pressure
on him, because I am acquainted with a bi
trans woman who thinks this is offensive, and
at risk of further offending her, I haven't asked
why, what's more, I'm a 20-year-old female
and a junior in college, and I am madly in love
with my girlfriend, yet I'm not particularly
fond of threesomes, but I go with the flow,
because I'm so afraid of rejection that I don't
even try anymore, so I'm up for anything
else—I would eat her out, piss on her,
whatever else—but not vaginal sex, what's
more I am wondering when the best time is to
mention being in an open relationship to new
girls, for I'm a gay guy in an open relationship
and I'm on Recon, a gay hookup/dating site
for guys into leather/fetish/BDSM, and I'm
not attracted to faggy men, because I'm a
female college student who's been dating the
sweetest, most attentive guy for about two
months, so you can guess that I'm a divorced
man and have been dating a married woman
in an open/poly relationship for six months,
and I am an intern at the health and wellness
center at my university, and I'm a 28-year-old
gay man, living with my partner for two years,

so I'm only going to say this once, also I'm in a
friends-with-benefits arrangement with a
woman I get along with really well, on top of
that I am interested in a real relationship, yet
I'm an 18-year-old male about to head off to
college in the fall, so needless to say that I'm
sensitive, just as I'm a gay dude who has been
trying to find an all-natural and organic lube,
and I'm 42, she's 39, yet I'm 16 and an openly
gay boy in a very welcoming community, but
I'm not polyamorous, as so many Seattleites
are, but I'm open-minded, in addition to that,
I am a 22-year-old female who's only ever
achieved orgasm during fellatio, and my
boyfriend will not perform fellatio on me, and
I am like any other woman in that I want a
husband and children, and he says he wants a
wife and kids, whereas I'm in a long-term
relationship with my partner; we've been
together for almost nine years, in a word, I'm
starting to feel guilty about doing this without
my dad's knowledge, on the other hand, I am
a 22-year-old male dating a wonderful 21-year-
old woman, and I'm just cruising for a few free
pictures and stories, so needless to say that
I'm trying to be responsible, so this weekend I
sat down and wrote my will, but I am now a

21-year-old woman who is moving toward a
healthy human sex life and trying to get over
what a sick kid I used to be, for I'm worried
this will lead to him suggesting we play in my
anal territory, and I am really uncomfortable
with this idea, which means that I am a
22-year-old straight male involved in a
yearlong relationship, and I am merely
curious to know if you've ever heard of this
and if you know why and how it happens,
also I'm happy to indulge him and have
started to enjoy it, yet I'm not a furry, but I
would like to surprise him and try this out, in
a word, I'm suffering from some sort of
carpal-tunnel/repetitive-motion/too-much-
beating-off injury, and it feels like my right
arm is on fire, and I am NOT turned on by
rape, whereas I'm ticklish, and I'm from the
other side of the country, what's more, I'm a bi
18 year old female, and I'm sitting in my lover's
San Francisco apartment wondering what I'm
doing, because I'm an escort and a pro
Domme, in a word, I'm now with a wonderful
guy who washes his beautiful cock daily and
wears clean, fresh undies, so I am looking for
a sexy hot female, and I'm a 28-year-old
heterosexual male with two questions, just as

I am a gay student at the University of Iowa
and there's this guy that I see on my way to
and from classes, in addition to that, I am a
nice healthy, handsome male in my late 20s,
and I've been single since coming out at age 16,
hence I'm in treatment for these things and
I've started going to a therapist, too, for I'm an
evangelical Christian in a country where that
is not a political statement, just as I'm
thrilled—I've always thought that the idea
that gay marriage could hurt straight people
was ridiculous, whereas I'm an outgoing guy
until I see a girl I'm interested in, on top of
that I'm casting my vote in hopes of creating a
viable third party, in a word, I'm in a
relationship with an awesome girl, for I'm a
24-year-old lesbian, and I have been with my
girlfriend for almost three years, on top of
that I'm a straight male, age 26, and I am a
20-year-old single white male who is straight,
a Christian, and pretty clean-cut, although
I'm also not thrilled that she's not GGG for me,
on the other hand, I'm a 30-year-old, mildly
genderqueer, bi-leaning-het male virgin, so
I'm a kinky, poly guy who meets awesome
kinky, poly girls on the internet, also I'm
writing on behalf of a friend of mine who is

too tired and disgusted to write, yet I am not
afraid of relationships, on the other hand, I'm
a 28-year-old woman, also I am 62 years old,
fit, handsome, and intelligent, and I'm sorry,
but dykes aren't chimps, and dykes don't have
to run off with men in order to breed, on top
of that I'm not stupid or evil, so I'm not
gonna DO anything, but I'm a 25-year-old who
is into pegging and think that this
characteristic could/should be seen as
attractive by women, in addition to that, I'm a
married straight man, just as I'm not upset
about your take on God, so you can guess
that I'm a 34-year-old openly gay white-collar
professional man in an open relationship with
my amazing boyfriend of nine years, although
I'm not as attracted to him when he isn't
dressed, and the sex isn't as exciting for me,
and I am fine with the act, but he produces a
high volume of ejaculate, like three
tablespoons' worth, which means that I am
always discovering more porn, underneath the
bed or tucked into drawers or hidden on a
shelf, in addition to that, I am a 24-year-old
hetero woman, so you can guess that I am a
24-year-old breeder female who can't figure
out what to call a turn-on of mine, but I'm

well-adjusted otherwise, a productive member
of society and all that, also I'm a gay black
male with a foot fetish, yet I'm a straight girl
in my early 20s and I've only had one sex
partner, for I'm confused and really just don't
know what to do about it, just as I am a
23-year-old female, and I'm not suggesting
that bisexual men can't be good husbands,
SBGB, and I am a straight female who has
been in a relationship for the last decade, in a
word, I'm ready to be monogamous, and I'm a
20-year-old straight girl, so I'm a fan, as
everyone knows, but anal sex isn't a litmus
test, yet I'm not sure, and I'm frustrated,
angry, and desperate, so you can guess that I
am going to hell, and I'm a girl in my mid-20s
living in a large city, although I'm a 20-year-
old female, which means that I'm a straight
woman who enjoys gay porn and writes slash
fiction, so needless to say that I'm unhappy
about it, on the other hand, I'm working on
my bachelor's and trying to get into graduate
school, what's more, I'm dating a woman who
happens to be another chap's wife, yet I'm gay
and a junior in high school, and I've had a
boyfriend for a year, hence I am so hurt and
broken-hearted that I can't sleep, and I'm torn

up thinking about this kid and want to do
something for him, hence I am discouraged,
but I am not getting one of those ridiculous
ball implants, in addition to that, I'm a gay
male in my late 20s and a survivor of
testicular cancer, just as I'm so confused, and
I'm stumped, on the other hand, I'm not
saying that everyone everywhere has to be
nonmonogamous; the authors of *Sex at Dawn*
don't make that argument either, so you can
guess that I'm a 21-year-old female and I
know the my-boyfriend-has-a-diaper-fetish
thing has been done to death, in a word, I'm
an early-20s gay guy turned on by hypnosis,
and I'm a 60-year-old white male, so you can
guess that I'm not, but I am writing in
reaction to the letter from Lonely and
Suicidal, who openly threatened you, which
means that I'm a normal guy with a dick that
sometimes gets hard when his woman isn't
around, in a word, I'm a 27-year-old straight
guy, and I've been in a monogamous
relationship with an awesome girl for four
years, yet I'm not sure how much ejaculate I'm
producing the second time I come, but it's
surely less than the first time, although I am
always up-front with my partners about this,

especially if I want to get serious with them,
so you can guess that I am a 21-year-old single
mother, for I'm well-read and well-spoken,
what's more, I am a 36-year-old gay man, so
I'm also worried that she will tell everyone we
know about my pegging kink, on the other
hand, I'm part of a live-in quad, and we all
raise our kids together, so I'm pretty far down
the polyamory rabbit hole, hence I'm a
17-year-old girl, just as I'm not invited to be
part of these girly encounters, also I'm a
bisexual woman who dated this amazing
beautiful bisexual guy, so you can guess that
I'm a 25-year-old bi girl in the Southwest, and
I've been with the same hetero guy for almost
three years, although I am a heterosexual
male, and I'm not going to vanish from his life
and leave him all happily ever after, and I'm
worried that if I let on that I recognize him
from his work, he might think I'm some crazy
stalker, so I'm off to collage now and in a
much biger city and nothing is better, because
I'm in a nonmonogamous marriage, whereas
I'm a 21-year-old woman, and I am continually
shocked by his ability and willingness to take
on new challenges in this department, in
addition to that, I am excited by the idea of

this, but I am scared I will end up feeling used, and I'm GGG and he's vanilla, on the other hand, I am a straight guy with a girlfriend and a problem, in a word, I am still beset by all manner of doubts and insecurities, what's more, I'm a man in my mid-30s, and I just started dating after the end of a five-year relationship, and I'm fine with being the secondary guy, although I am engaged to a man whose sexual orientation is somewhat confusing to me, just as I am currently single, and I'm a 21-year-old gay male, but I'm a longtime fan and agree with you 99 percent of the time, and I'm usually annoyed when you run letters from angry readers, although I'm inclined to never speak of it again unless she does first, so you can guess that I am adjusting to a truth I had long suspected, but I'm a gay man living in San Francisco, so you can guess that I am now doing well in therapy, much improvement in recent months, although I am a 21-year-old gay male, whereas I'm artsy, on the other hand, I'm a 24-year-old female living in London, where I have just finished a degree in circus arts, so I'm going to stick this in my urethra, in addition to that, I'm a girl with a

low libido, but I'm left blue balled for fear of
hurting her further, and she feels bad for not
having me finish, so needless to say that I'm
not going to tie up this line over a fictitious
story, she snapped, just as I'm curious to hear
your opinion and am hoping you will supply
me with an intelligent retort, which means
that I'm a 25-year-old straight female, just as
I'm a 21-year-old female with a 20-year-old
boyfriend, on the other hand, I'm a
thirtysomething gay male who's attracted to
married men, yet I am a 45-year-old
heterosexual male, and I'm a straight man,
although I'm straight, he'll tell himself, I was
seduced, for I'm confused, but I'm GGG, and
he's gotten really good about taking initiative
and suggesting things, although I'm afraid
that I'm happily married, but if I'm into
stretch marks, someone else out there must
be, so I'm a woman in my mid-40s, married
more than two decades, which means that I
am horrified, but strangely aroused, so you
can guess that I'm speaking as a mom myself
now, because I'm 23, straight, and female, and
I'm a smoker and my boyfriend has a smoking
fetish, although I am a mid-20s straight
woman who dates a lot, yet I'm a 24-year-old

male with a 28-year-old girlfriend, and I'm
writing about the advice you gave last week to
the woman faced with the prospect of raising
her baby alone, for I'm happier now than I
ever thought possible, on the other hand, I'm
a 20-year-old bi girl and I've been with my
boyfriend a little over a year, so I'm on
vacation right now, and I am deeply in love
with this guy and want more out of our
relationship, however, I do respect him and
would never out him, although I'm a gay man
in a relationship for two years, and I am still
in shock and not quite sure how to deal with
it, just as I am his first strap-on girlfriend, so
I am thinking about modifying a toy in a way
that might enable her to squirt up my ass, so I
am a lesbian who recently graduated from
college, and I'm not hurting anyone, but this
seems wrong, on the other hand, I'm not
talking through it, like a piercing, but into it,
going in at the head and moving down into
the shaft, in addition to that, I am a 33-year-
old male who got back in touch with an old
college girlfriend (now married), and I am
looking for a woman to give me an enema, so
you can guess that I'm having an interesting
dilemma, because I'm a het male professional

in my mid-20s who wants to find a female
dominant partner, on top of that I'm a
51-year-old woman, also I'm sensitive,
fashionable, and artistic, and she tells me she's
more attracted to the all-American-man type,
on the other hand, and I am a single hetero
male, and I'm not saying I want him to piss on
me or strangle me, Dan, but I'm adventurous,
and let him do it once, and I'm funny,
independent, and easygoing, because I am a
26-year-old lesbian in a relationship with a
21-year-old, on top of that I'm I am soooo wet
already, hence I'm a recovering anorexic and I
am still struggling a great deal to eat normal
and healthy portions of food, and I'm an idiot,
in addition to that, I'm a 41-year-old straight
woman, although I'm not looking to blame
his weight gain for my libido issues, just as I
am dating a Japanese girl who is so into
keeping her pubic area hair-free that she
actually plucks the hairs out, in a word, I'm a
29-year-old woman and a journalist in my
country, Italy, and I've been going out with my
boyfriend for four years, so you can guess that
I am mourning the loss of intimacy and
connection with another person, in a word,
I'm a 21-year-old female, so I'm just being, you

know, scientific and everything, on the other hand, I'm happily married, have two children, and live in a completely different part of the country now, which means that I'm a 22-year-old female, and the older I get, the more often I am ridiculed by straight men for being ugly, and I'm not totally against the idea, hence I'm in college and I write a sex/relationship column for the campus newspaper, just as I'm the first person he has ever shared his kinks with: age regression/diapers/submission, so I'm not monogamous and I can't choose to be monogamous, although I'm a 27-year-old woman in a committed relationship, yet I found myself alone for a long period of time, so needless to say that I'm a huge fan of yours, and I know that you've had some issues reconciling your own life with loved ones within the Catholic Church, because I am underage and too young to experiment and I wouldn't feel comfortable experimenting anyway since I don't know what I am, but I'm a 19-year-old newbie lesbian Dom starting a relationship with a smart, sexy, wildly kinky 22-year-old, and I'm not sure what he's doing to me, but I am willing to give it time and effort, accept my faults, and breathe deeply

rather than react in anger when we talk
through things, in addition to that, I am a
21-year-old straight girl, and I wanted to
thank you, and I'm probably overreacting due
to all the extra hormones, because I am a
straight male who has never been in a
romantic relationship, so needless to say that I
am marrying the amazing bi guy with a
cuckold fetish and I couldn't be happier, and I
am a modern single mother, so I'm 25 pounds
lighter now thanks to her honesty (and a
heart scare), and I am also reexploring my bi
attractions, so I am 50 and a lesbian, but I'm
in college now; we've been dating since high
school, on top of that I'm a 28-year-old gay
male who recently attended a sporting event
in the beautiful city of Portland, Oregon, but
I'm not going to change my mind, because I
am curious what you think about sneaky
facials, on the other hand, I'm simultaneously
creeped out and intrigued, on top of that I'm
a 25-year-old straight guy, and I'm extremely
courageous that way, although I'm queer and
mostly into women, but with a severe
attraction to one particular guy, although I'm
a 16-year-old gay boy, on the other hand, I'm a
23-year-old female college student whose life

consists of going to class and going to the
gym, although I'm freaking out, whereas I'm
16 and gay, so needless to say that I am a
woman in my early 20s and I have been in a
happy hetero relationship for several years,
yet I'm too young for breast-reduction
surgery or gender-reassignment counseling,
but these are things I'm considering, hence
I'm a 17-year-old gay male, whereas I'm a
19-year-old girl, attractive, outgoing, and
ambitious, and I'm not talking about 'leaving'
her, although I'm 99 percent sure it's her, so
you can guess that I'm a heterosexual male,
and I'm more sane than most, in a word, I'm
an American college student, and I am a
person in the public eye—let's just say I'm in
politics—and can't risk the whole world
knowing, although I'm very clean and take
great pride in my apartment, in addition to
that, I am a pretty GGG kind of gal, on top of
that I'm so angry, because I'm a (mostly)
straight male and I've been dating the same
woman for more than a year, in addition to
that, I am 28, female, and bi, yet I'm also
shamefully awkward around him now, so
needless to say that I'm the bisexual everyone
loves to hate because I want to be in a poly

relationship with both a man and a woman,
and I'm 30 and married, on the other hand,
I'm not in the best shape, which means that I
am a virgin—both genders considered—and
the idea of sex right now makes me uneasy,
yet I am a professional dominatrix located in
Boston, so I'm pretty sure if I found a woman
interested in an affair or a FWB situation, it
would be a much riskier emotional tightrope,
although I'm 26, straight, and male, yet I'm
somewhat of a novice to the whole back-
porch scene, but all of my adventures have
ended up with santorum everywhere, just as
I'm a gay man who is about to turn 35, what's
more, I am a 30-year-old straight man who
has always known that he is a poly, and I'm
about to visit a friend who used to be my
boyfriend and who has been my lover when
we've visited each other since, in a word, I'm
afraid to even look around his house because I
might see something that will tell me he's
lying, which means that I am mostly okay
with this: I take care of myself as necessary,
but I am a 23-year-old woman, which means
that I am obsessed with this guy in my class,
so you can guess that I'm in a crisis, on top of
that I'm not interested in being anyone's

sperm donor at the moment, although I am currently separated, and I'm stumped and worried I won't be able to make this happen for him, on the other hand, I am an open bisexual male, and my friend is straight, so you can guess that I am a really kinky person: I've been very sexually active and into BDSM since I was 16, hence I'm 26, Caucasian, and in good health, so I am a 23-year-old woman, and I am a girl who sabotaged my relationship, on top of that I am very enthusiastic about sex, and very vocal and demanding, but I am a hard-working, 25-year-old guy down on his luck, Dan, so needless to say that I'm intrigued, and I'm a 33-year-old lesbian, so I'm a young-adult gay virgin, also I'm wondering how you display the desk, and if you write at it, in a word, I'm really into the idea of being sprayed with my wife's breast milk, although I'm trying not to put pressure on her, so you can guess that I'm a 46-year-old homo who's fairly content most days living the single life, hence I am desperate for ideas on how to make this better, because I'm female, bi, mid-20s, into kink—bedroom-only BDSM stuff—and involved in the local kink scene in NYC, also I'm swimming in

unfamiliar waters here with no life vest, and
I'm sure you can see where this is going,
because I'm a 25-year-old gay male with a foot
fetish, on top of that I'm worried that my son
may not know how to say no to him, and I'm
a 32-year-old female engaged to a 34-year-old
man, so needless to say that I'm a partnered
gay man who happens to have a small cock,
although I am a decent-looking, educated, and
almost young gay man; I am also a
Republican, and I'm not happy with the
restrictions, but I can't ask for more because
she gets so depressed talking about it, yet I'm
a smart, professional woman in my mid-30s
who dates the same, on top of that I'm a fan
of stable, loving, committed, opposite-sex
relationships, and I am bisexual and work in
marketing for the adult industry, on the other
hand, I'm the very portrait of an average
American woman, a vanilla kind of girl, also I
am disturbd by naked pic bribing you admittd
& encouraged in yr last column, on the other
hand, I'm a gay man who has been seeing a
devout Christian gay guy for one year, so I am
struggling with my reaction to this, hence I'm
curious because I've shared apartments with
straight guys and it's never been a problem,

whereas I'm not sure if I'm being judgmental
and superficial, because I am a 48-year-old
gay man and have been in a committed and
monogamous relationship with a wonderful
man for 20 years, and I'm sorry, but I'm the
other woman to a man 14 years my senior, so
you can guess that I'm not seeing this guy
anymore, and I am wondering if you think
that lesbians might be more open-minded in
assisting me in my transition, although I am
33 and my sister is 40, and I'm writing
because I need your help, hence I'm also a
mother, and I'm a straight male who skipped
the sleeping around phase and went straight
to long-term boyfriend, but I am a single
woman with a high libido, also I'm a 17-year-
old male and I'm currently in a relationship
with a girl who was sexually active before we
got together, what's more, I'm in a decent-to-
great marriage, have two kids, a good life,
which means that I'm always disappointed
when your column doesn't deal with bizarre
sexual practices, also I'm a 28-year-old
straight female, just as I'm about to turn 21,
and I've been with a great guy for over a year,
what's more, I am openly gay, he is closeted,
so I'm a 17-year-old male with a tickling fetish

and I don't have a problem with it, which
means that I'm so used to this stuff, he said,
it's nothing new to me, so you can guess that I
am a leather daddy in a big city, although I'm
19, in the army, and in the closet, on the other
hand, I'm female, early 40s, and I like to
watch, because I'm an adopted gay boy who
was thrown for a loop when I was tracked
down by two younger brothers I never knew I
had, on top of that I'm a 25-year-old lesbian,
and I live with my partner of two years, what's
more, I am a single straight girl, and I'm also a
politically connected woman, a very in control
type, and when I say no I mean no, so I'm a
24-year-old guy, and my wife and I have been
married for two years, and I'm concerned
about this affecting my sex life, what's more, I
am a white, 21-year-old lesbian girl, so you can
guess that I'm a 24-year-old female and I've
just started seeing a great guy, which means
that I'm a 32-year-old woman, married for
seven years, and I have slept with three men
and one woman since marrying my husband,
and I'm a woman, said Mistress Matisse, a
writer, professional dominatrix, and sex-
workers-rights activist, hence I'm a gay guy,
25, in great shape, no STDs, because I am

super-in-love with a wonderful woman who I
hope to spend the rest of my life with, in
addition to that, I'm a 38-year-old straight
male in a long-term relationship, so you can
guess that I am a 24-year-old lesbian, so I'm
talking about your typical random hookup at
a bar, party, or dorm room, although I am a
30-year-old woman with a strange problem,
because I am successful, intelligent, ambitious,
kind, and better than average in the looks
department, on the other hand, I'm a
transman—so a two-inch micropenis actually
sounds pretty damn good, which means that
I'm a 25-year-old straight man, yet I am very
conflicted about how to proceed, on the other
hand, I'm very attracted to a girl who has had
a very large number of sexual partners,
whereas I am a 30-year-old female with a
live-in boyfriend, and I'm attractive and I
notice guys checking me out—making the
gym a second home does have benefits, hence
I am an adult hetero woman, and I have a
recurring fantasy that gives me pause, so I am
curious what you or your readers think,
although I'm not going to ask you to compare
our pics, but is there a concrete checklist to
verify if someone is out of your league, in a

word, I'm a 25-year-old straight male, and I
love to go down on women, also I'm a GGG
38-year-old single woman, longtime reader,
first-time writer, what's more, I'm dating a guy
who didn't bother to squirrel away the porn in
his bathroom the first time I came over, and I
am so done, so you can guess that I'm an
18-year-old male in my first serious
relationship, whereas I am thinking about
taking an ad out in a local paper, but what
about safety, on the other hand, I'm an
18-year-old gal and have never had sex with
another person, but I do get off on my own,
just as I'm 20 and have been in a relationship
for two years, and I am writing to thank you,
and I am a single female, on the other hand,
I'm a bit out of your usual demographic,
age-wise (I'm 70), but I am still an avid reader,
just as I'm a 21-year-old straight male, and I'm
mildly autistic, but I am not one of them, in a
word, I'm a merrily married straight woman
with an amazing husband and what was once
a thriving sex life, so you can guess that I'm
not perfect, but I've bent over backwards to be
a good guy and make this work, and I'm very
much in love with my wife, in addition to that,
I am a crossdresser currently going through

feminization training with an internet
Mistress, which means that I'm an actor in
New York and I'm interested in developing a
theater piece that explores the world of
fetishes, but I'm a little uneasy about this for
disease-related and psychological reasons, and
also because I'm a virgin, on top of that I'm an
18-year-old hetero male college student,
whereas I'm a bisexual woman, age 20, and I
am threesome-ing it with my best friend and
her boyfriend during a stay abroad, but I'm
sick of his complaining, also I'm a 17-year-old
high-school student, male, into foot worship
and humiliation, and I'm mooning over this
guy who works in a store up the street from
my house, on the other hand, I am a full-time
student training to become a nurse, so I'm
serious, which means that I'm a 43-year-old
woman, married for 19 years, and I need your
help, just as I'm intersex, but I identify as
female, so you can guess that I'm a 27-year-
old straight guy who's been in an open
relationship for six years, and I am a nice-
looking man who enjoys sex very much,
because I'm a straight 26-year-old diaper
lover, hence I'm more of a vanilla kind of
dude, but in the spirit of being GGG, I've been

doing this for her, what's more, I'm a 22-year-old gay male, and I'm in my 30s, and I've had a fair bit of sexual experience, so you can guess that I'm so happy, I could cry, for I am a 32-year-old woman with a loving boyfriend of just over a year, whereas I'm very miserable, frustrated, and lonely, also I am a woman who is with the love of her life, so I'm 19 years old and gay and a virgin, in a word, I'm a smooth-talking guy in some ways, and I am currently a senior in high school, but come Saturday, I will be a high-school grad, on top of that I'm a 28-year-old, professional, single woman, and I am a fairly successful man, whereas I'm a 40-year-old guy who strongly prefers sex with women to men (percentage-wise I'm 70/30), also I'm pro-sex, bisexual, and GGG, but I am 24 years old and lost my entire glans penis, the head of my dick, in a botched circumcision, on top of that I'm a 26-year-old queer woman, and I'm hoping that guys, in general, don't give a damn about pussy farts if the sex was good, what's more, I am writing because I recently found out that my dad has a problem with online porn, which means that I'm a 19-year-old male college student, and I am thinking of buying some sex toys to use

while I work to overcome my problems, so
I'm glad you're there to let people know that
it's all going to be okay, in a word, I'm a
28-year-old pan-curious married guy from the
Midwest about to move to San Francisco, but
I'm very attracted to one of my teachers, also
I'm a 22-year-old queer chick who came out
only a couple years ago, yet I'm intelligent,
attractive, and have a great sense of humor, on
top of that I am trying to understand some
fantasies I have, because I am a 21-year-old,
attractive straight male with an identical twin
brother, also straight, which means that I'm
scared at the beginning of the fantasy, but by
the end, I succumb to the erotic power of
their undulating appendages, and I am so out
of here, although I am addressing this to
both, on top of that I'm a guy, and I'm a
hetero college male and I recently started
dating a hetero college female, whereas I am a
32-year-old male, and I am an overweight gay
boy from Rhode Island, and I'm hoping we
can be friends in the future, just as I'm a
loving guy and I can deal with it, so needless
to say that I'm an 18-year-old female college
student in New York, average weight,
attractive in the face, and I'm good-looking, I

guess, because really hot guys are always
hitting on me, so I'm a gorgeous 23-year-old
male that could easily have won your tighty-
whitey contest, also I am 26 years old and in a
respectful but super-sexual relationship with a
recent divorcée in her 40s, and I'm responsible
and successful, and I don't smoke that often,
hence I'm a girl that REALLY enjoys being
fisted by my boyfriend, also I am a 28-year-
old married straight male, in addition to that,
I am a bisexual woman recently out of a long-
term relationship, and I am interested in
joining this little playgroup, but I'm not a
bad-looking guy, in addition to that, I'm a
21-year-old student, and I'm a Femme Dom
who loves ropes, while he's pretty vanilla, so
needless to say that I am also a submissive
crossdresser with a domestication fetish, just
as I'm a 52-year-old gay man—native San
Franciscan—who lost count of the friends I
buried from AIDS, so I am sick of this, and I'm
an 18-year-old straight female, in addition to
that, I'm a straight teenage male, but I can't
climax unless I am stimulating my anus or
rectum, although I'm not overweight, I've
been told my whole life how good-looking I
am, and my boyfriend tells me he loves my

body, on the other hand, I'm a straight male in my early 20s who has so far chosen to remain a virgin, so I am completely shocked, as we have an intimate and loving relationship, yet I'm 21, female, and pretty experienced, on the other hand, I am a black man who enjoys drinking the piss of other black males, what's more, I'm artsy, and I'm also a mother, yet I'm uncomfortable not disclosing my HIV status, hence I'm so angry, but I'm straight, and she asked me if I wanted to be in it, with or without my boyfriend of two years, so you can guess that I am a single professional gal who likes to party, because I'm a straight woman, also I'm a middle-aged guy, more twisted than most, and I'm a large-breasted man, on top of that I'm also a CUDDLE ADDICT, just as I'm the president of NAMBLA, yet I'm a straight, 26-year-old, relatively kinky male, in a word, I'm a balanced bisexual male in a good marriage, which means that I'm an asshole, I suppose, but there it is, on top of that I'm a sadist, and I'm afraid to read the advice you're going to give me, also I'm sensitive, which means that I'm a 200% straight guy, married with children, and I'm a 26-year-old guy in a polyamorous relationship, yet I'm a gay man

in my mid-20s with an etiquette question,
because I'm a married man with the usual
three-way fantasies, so I'm dumbfounded, and
I'm a theater person, yet I'm not sure what
you mean by that, so I'm leaving, because I'm
the cleanest kid in town, on the other hand,
I'm a 25-year-old guy with a gender-neutral
partner, which means that I'm a straight
female with my own boyfriend, so I'm torn,
yet I'm a happy, healthy fat chick, and I'm a
middle-aged, fat, and happy gay man, on the
other hand, I'm a slut, too, so I'm a little
traumatized, also I'm a submissive gay boy
into puppy play, what's more, I'm an introvert
and a private person, which means that I'm a
dyke, but I'll do boys, too, on top of that I'm
an actor in New York City, because I'm a
porn-positive woman in my 30s, and I'm hurt,
just as I'm an early-40s gal living in the
Midwest, hence I'm an escort and a pro
Domme, on top of that I'm among the
growing legions of cuckold fetishists, and I'm
a lost little lesbian, which means that I'm a
Roman Catholic, hence I'm in a bad place,
what's more, I'm about 5-feet, 6-inches tall
and weigh 103 pounds, yet I'm an average guy,
not a big stud, hence I'm stumped, and I'm a

15-year-old male in need of advice, and I'm
going to jail for this, also I'm a gay college
student who's into bondage and kink, so I'm
intrigued, just as I'm a 42-year-old gay man
with a superhero fetish, yet I'm a zoophile
and always have been, what's more, I'm a gay
guy, and I'm a straight guy who has the same
desires, in a word, I'm confused, hence I'm a
young lesbian with the ability to ejaculate,
which means that I'm in shock, and I'm a
22-year-old male with a vaginal fisting fetish,
what's more, I'm a top, and I'm a supporter, in
a word, I'm afraid we're playing with fire,
which means that I'm a smoker and my
partner is a nonsmoker, yet I'm a student and
can't afford too much of this, because I'm a
woman and I masturbate, on the other hand,
I'm a romantic guy, menstrual cycles don't
bother me, but I'm a freakin' lesbian, just as
I'm not a prude, in a word, I'm an 18-year-old
girl in a small town in Tennessee, so I'm really
pissed, and I'm sorry for the length of this
letter, but it's the only sex problem we have,
on the other hand, I'm a 37-year-old single
father with a 14-year-old son, hence I'm
freaking out, yet I'm a well-built body
builder/actor, and I'm getting sick of this

inner dialogue, what's more, I'm a 26-year-old
fag with a common problem, but I'm also a
grandmother, which means that I'm an ethical
encourager, damnit, and I'm a man who gets
off on women hypnotizing men, and I'm an
idiot, because I'm ticklish, so I'm disappointed
in myself, because I'm a healthy 26-year-old
girl and I really like sex, and I'm unhappy
about it, on the other hand, I'm a 17-year-old
breeder chick, and I'm not ugly, but I'm just
too damn horny, and I'm a woman who wants
to be spanked, yet I'm a hetero guy who wears
thong underwear, and I'm not crazy, so I'm
inclined to let it be, also I'm a very good-
looking gay boi, yet I'm an American college
student, so I'm desperate, also I'm a middle-
aged guy, and I'm a female college student and
a feminist, on top of that I'm a girl who wants
to wake up my guy with a blowjob, so I'm a
53-year-old woman, but I'm sorry, and I'm a
youth who identifies as asexual, on top of that
I'm a twentysomething professional snow-
boarder, but I'm troubled, Dan, and I'm also
physically aching at memories of fucking my
ex, and I'm falling apart.

All "Savage Love" sex advice columns by Dan Savage from thestranger.com/columns/savage-love; retrieved June 2015; approx. 1 million tokens at 34,000 types.

Sentences beginning with "I am" or "I'm" were concatenated with conjunctions such as "but," "yet," "on the other hand," etc.

A very short excerpt of this work appeared in: Hannes Bajohr, TIMIDITIES (Berlin: Readux, 2015), and online at theoffingmag.com.

In collaboration with Gregor Weichbrodt, a German version using a corpus of parship.com profiles appeared in Edit 70/2016 under the title "Über mich selbst."

With thanks to Amanda DeMarco for her support and encouragement.

Impressum

Hannes Bajohr ist Teil des Textkollektivs OXOA.
www.oxoa.li | *www.hannesbajohr.de*

Dies ist ein Titel der Reihe FROHMANN/OXOA.

© 2016 by Hannes Bajohr und Frohmann Verlag,
Christiane Frohmann, Berlin.
frohmann.orbanism.com

ISBN Paperback: 978-3944195438

Die Deutsche Nationalbibliothek verzeichnet diese Publikation in der Deutschen Nationalbibliografie; detaillierte bibliografische Daten sind im Internet über http://dnb.d-nb.de abrufbar.

www.ingramcontent.com/pod-product-compliance
Lightning Source LLC
Chambersburg PA
CBHW060405030726
47497CB00003B/853